The Below: Phillipe's Revenge

First Printing, 2022

Imprint: Imagine Nation

Imagine Nation

Chenoa, IL 61726

AuthorJenniferLush@gmail.com

Chapter One

Stowaway

The timing couldn't be worse, but Roark couldn't do anything about it. He inched along on the cobblestone road which would lead to the stairway down to the canal, only he wouldn't venture that far. He had to stick to the shadows.

As he crept closer, he could hear the men working on the dock below. His heart rate increased. He would've noticed a shaking in his hands if they weren't clenched in fists around the gunny sack he was carrying. This was the last cargo ship scheduled out of port for weeks, and he needed to make sure he was on it.

The baby was due any day now, and he hated the idea of leaving Esther and his child behind. It was only temporary. They had enough money saved to secure his safe passage, or to provide for Esther and their child for a couple months until he settled somewhere new.

Even worse, he had left her a note detailing his plans instead of talking to her face to face. If he had talked to her about it, she would've done everything she could to prevent him from leaving. He couldn't bear to see her heart break when he ultimately left anyway.

The Below ordered all creatures to leave the city by the end of the month. It wasn't safe for them here anymore. Several had been discovered recently and had been violently killed. Everyone in town was on high alert. Everyone suspected the young and old alike of not being human.

The Above Guard would gather up anyone who didn't leave town by month's end. They would be sent back to the Below. Once you were sent back down, you would almost never be allowed to come to the surface again.

Stowing away on this ship tonight was his one real chance. Esther would be protected. They wouldn't force her to leave with a newborn. They'd give her three months additional stay to prepare. That had been the way since he first came to the Above. The extension would apply to him as well, but they'd be no better off at the end of it.

If he left now, he'd be able to send for her by the end of the extension. Roark was certain he could manage it sooner.

Roark watched the men on the dock loading the crates and bags onto the ship through the trees along the street. He stepped inside the foliage that grew on the hill between the canal and the road. It was time to begin his descent downward until the right moment presented itself to hide amongst the cargo.

He had barely made it off the road when he heard her. She must have woken in the night and found the letter he left on the table when he wasn't in bed. This could ruin everything. He stepped out from the brush and saw her. She was still about fifty yards away. One hand was cupping her oversized belly, and she struggled to walk.

The sailors were still busy with their tasks and oblivious to the emotional woman headed their way. He dropped his burlap bag and took off running in her direction. If she came much closer yelling like that, she would surely be disruptive enough to distract them.

When he met up with her, he angrily said, "Be quiet," in a hushed voice. "Are you trying to get me discovered?"

Roark regretted the words as soon as he spoke them. He knew she wouldn't want anything to happen to him.

Esther was in tears. Wet streaks streamed down her face. She had been crying for a stretch. "Of course not! Just don't leave me."

"I could never leave you," Roark told her. "This is only for the interim. You're not thinking clearly right now. Go home and get some rest. In the morning, you will see this had to be done."

"Wait until after our child is born," she begged.

The crushing pain he felt from causing her such distress had to be ten times worse than the hurt he caused, but there was no other way. "Let me go. I'll find work. I'm skilled," he reminded her. "I can sleep and forage in the woods to save every cent until I have enough money. It won't take long I promise. If I stay, I won't be able to manage to provide for all three of us and cover the expenses of our travel."

She shook her head. The tears flowed more violently making it harder for her to speak. "You can't!" she cried. "You can't leave now."

Another much louder shout escaped from her lips, and she doubled over in pain. She gripped her belly with both hands and moaned.

'*Oh, no,*' Roark thought. '*Her labors have started.*'

This can't be happening. He was almost out of time. The sailors would make quick work of loading the boat. He needed to get down to the dock. It was time to say goodbye. He touched his forehead to her protruding belly and rubbed either side of it with his hands.

She ran her fingers through his hair and pleaded with him. "Stay. Please stay with me."

Roark stepped back and took her hands in his, kissing the back of each one gently. "If there was any other way, I would," he told her. "I love you," he said, running back down the road toward the canal.

He could hear her shuffling along behind him, calling his name until she let out a cry when another pain overtook her. There wasn't much time before she caught the attention of the sailors.

The gunny sack lay near the road where he dropped it. He picked it up and disappeared into the brush never looking back. The foliage was thick there which is why he chose that point to sneak down the hill. He made his way as quickly as possible while still being careful not to make too much noise or risk falling.

There was no time to hesitate. He had to get into position before the sailors finished loading the boat. Plus he now had to beat Esther's arrival.

At the edge of the brush, he let his eyes adjust to the darkness. The sailors had lanterns displayed on the dock. They shone around them, aiding their work. He could see their intense focus in getting their tasks done. Two men grabbed a crate and carried it across the wooden plank bridge to the boat.

That's when he made his move. He darted straight ahead and hid behind one of the few remaining crates. At not quite four foot tall, he only needed to bow his head to hide.

Esther was drawing closer. Her voice was still faint, but he could hear it because he was listening for her. She would soon be close enough for the sailors to take notice. If they rushed to the aid of a pregnant woman in distress, he hoped they would chalk up her claims that her hydrohomunculus husband was trying to stow away on their boat to nothing more than labor related hysteria. She was scared and alone, hurt and betrayed, and in a lot of pain. There was no doubt the words could fall from her mouth without a second thought.

Roark peeked around the crate at the pile of gunny sacks waiting to be loaded. One sailor was tossing them on the boat, and he stood fairly close to the captain while he worked.

He stepped inside the sack he brought with him, pulling it up close to his shoulders. Once both men were looking away, he shimmied to the closest edge of the pile, pulled the sack over his head, and flopped onto the rest of the load.

Even with the illumination of the lanterns, it would be difficult for any of the sailors to notice the rising and falling of his chest beneath the burlap barrier in the darkness. He lay perfectly still trying to slow his breathing willfully, not wanting to take the chance of being found.

Esther's voice was still distant. It sounded farther away as it traveled through the sack to reach his ears. He could still tell she was getting closer. Her words were more distinguishable now.

Once he was on the boat, he could find a new place to hide. He just needed to get on deck. That's when he felt the tug.

He was weightless in the air. Everything went in slow motion. For a fleeting second, he felt peace. All thoughts of Esther who was laboring with their child, nearing the canal, and would soon draw the attention of the sailors had left his mind. He no longer feared being caught. The boat would provide a multitude of places for him to hide with his small stature. When you're looking for someone, you tend to search for a person who stands at eye level, not someone who wouldn't reach your waist.

His plan had come to fruition. Soon he and his family would be safe. Esther may never forgive him for leaving her like this, but he would spend the rest of her life making it up to her.

Then the fleeting second ended, and he realized the trajectory was wrong. He was no longer flying up through the air toward the boat. He was falling down. Roark hadn't been airborne long enough to be safely landing on board. He braced himself for the hard impact of landing with a thud on the dock, but it never happened.

He kept falling and falling. It felt like minutes had passed although he was aware it had only been a couple seconds since the sailor lifted him in the air. When something finally broke his fall, it was soft and gentle. It wasn't the painful landing he was expecting.

Roark didn't feel the water at first, but he heard the

splash.

"I'm sorry, sir," the muffled voice of the sailor said. "I wasn't expecting it to be heavy."

"Heavy?" the commander asked with surprise in his voice.

Roark wondered how long the sack might keep him safe from the water that surrounded him, but he didn't need to contemplate it for long. No sooner had the thought entered his mind that perhaps the burlap would keep the water out then he felt the wetness on his legs. Survival instincts took over. He took a deep breath and fought to free himself from the sack. If he could make it to the other side of the canal and out of the water, he might have a chance.

Blinding green and yellow lights shot out around him. He was taking on too much water at once. The chemical changes in his body caused by it were happening in rapid fire succession, and they gave off an energy that in large amounts created light. It would be impossible for him to hide with the beams giving away his location. He had to get out of the canal before they closed in on him.

Once he made it to dry land, the light effects would cease. He could run and hide, and he could potentially save himself. In the water, it was him disadvantaged against the entire crew. They would have no trouble finding him in the darkness with the lights radiating from his body, marking the spot where they should attack. Before he could quickly surface for another breath of air, he felt the first blow.

Chapter Two

Childbirth

Esther was almost to the stairs when she heard the sound of something splashing in the water. It wasn't her intention to bring any harm to Roark. She had hoped if she could catch the sailors' attention, they would come to the aid of a pregnant woman in distress. It would slow the loading of the boat, and perhaps make it impossible for Roark to get away. All she wanted to do was keep him with her.

When she heard the gurgle of the burlap bag taking on water, she cried out in misery and dropped to the ground. Between the pain of her labor and her heartbreak, she no longer had the strength to stay on her feet. It was close now. The baby was coming. The fear that her presence had caused the distraction that sent her husband into the canal was overwhelming. She knew it was Roark because the lights sparkled across the canal almost immediately after she heard the sound of his body breaking the surface.

She regretted leaving the house to look for him. If she had just stayed home, she wouldn't be bringing a child into the world while listening to her husband's demise. The trees next to her blocked the view of what was happening alongside the dock, but it didn't stop the sounds from reaching her.

There were the soft but unmistakable hums as sailors unsheathed their swords, and the swishing noises they made as the sailors plunged them into the water hoping to find their target. Roark tried to surface, gasping for breath and screaming out in pain. The sailors shouted to each other.

"Get him!"

"Don't let it escape!"

"What is it?"

"It doesn't belong here!"

"Kill it!"

The green and yellow lights that managed to shine through the openings of the intertwined branches were the only proof she had that Roark was still alive. They provided enough light for her to see the ripples spreading across the canal caused by her husband's struggle and the purplish gray rock that jutted out of the far side of the water.

She bent her legs, spread her knees, and began to push. The screams she emitted cut through the darkness, but the sailors didn't hear them. The lights disappeared, and she knew Roark was gone.

"Where is it?"

"I've got him."

There were grunting noises as the men pulled Roark's body from the water and flopped it on the dock. They cheered and congratulated each other on their victory.

Esther pushed again. Her wails were a mixture of child birth pain, grief, guilt, regret and heartache. They echoed under the canal bridge, amplifying her cries, and reverberating them back to her multiple times over.

The sailors were too caught up in their revelry. They never gave her notice, but it wouldn't stay that way for long. Soon her cries of pain would break through to them. If not hers, then the cries of a newborn would most definitely catch their interest.

She couldn't worry about what would happen then. If they suspected she had any involvement with the beast they killed in the water, she would suffer the same fate along with her child. In her weakened state, she wouldn't be able to stand up without a struggle, much less run from the men. Those thoughts didn't linger long. She couldn't think beyond her pain.

With one final push, her baby was born. She looked down and saw a beautiful baby boy. Roark had wanted a son so desperately. She was captivated by this tiny, perfect creature laying between her legs. That's why she didn't discern the rock had moved.

The men began shouting again. They were frantic and afraid. It couldn't be her or her child that caused them alarm. There was no way they could be perceived as a threat to the sailors.

She turned her head toward the trees, hoping beyond all probability that Roark was still alive. He had played dead and ran the first chance he had. It would still leave her in danger of being discovered by the crew on the dock below her, but the slim chance that her love had made it was already renewing her strength.

Even in the darkness, she noticed the shadow that crept

over her. She looked to the canal and saw the purplish gray monster rising out of the water. It resembled a dragon with its long wings partially folded at its side. The face was long with a protruding snout, and its head was turned just slightly enough to be able to view the crest in the back. There was something that was as oddly beautiful about it as it was hideous. It was at least a story high with part of it still submerged beneath the water. It was coming directly at her.

Tales of sea monsters had been told since man first voyaged the sea. The question of if they were real or fantasy was up to the listener to decide. Sailors believed they were real. Esther learned they were real after meeting Roark. He had tales without end of the various creatures that lived amongst the humans, but she had never heard of sea monsters or dragons being inside the village.

The closer the creature got to her the more distant the sailors' voices sounded to her frightened mind. It was like her tunnel vision that focused on the water dragon also muffled any noises that weren't in her direct line of sight. They hadn't moved. They were frozen in terror. They wanted to attack, but were unable to move a muscle.

The creature swooped down on her, and she screamed. It was a blood curdling final scream before death, but the monster didn't attack. It moved back as quickly as it had come for her, and straightened up in the water. The dragon's mouth was nestled inside of its wing. The bottom jaw could be seen moving up and down.

Esther looked at the road between her legs. Her son was gone. The last thought she had before passing out was the beast was eating her child.

Chapter Three

Water Dragon

Kayda opened her one eye above the surface and watched the whole scene unfold. It was only a matter of time before the human men directed their attention to the woman giving birth. If they had even an ounce of suspicion she was connected to the hydrohomunculus they had just killed, the baby would be in danger. Her maternal instincts urged her to do something to help, but it would come at a cost. Showing herself in front of all these people even in the defense of a helpless babe would find her banished to the Below.

When the first sailor turned his attention toward the woman on the road, it pushed all thoughts of consequence from her mind. Kayda no longer considered the repercussions of intervening. She rose from the water and towered over the new mother. She wished she could communicate with this woman. No harm would come to her baby. She was there to help.

The panic in the mother's eyes made Kayda wince. There was nothing evil about her, but it was always everyone's first assumption.

Kayda dove to the road and tucked the baby human hybrid in the crook of her wing. She sat up in the water and looked at the little boy. He didn't appear to be breathing. She blew softly in his face, and the boy reacted with a low cry. At least she didn't make her presence known for nothing. She chewed through the cord extending from his belly and singed it lightly with her fire as she had watched humans do when they gave birth on the water.

She gave one last look to the baby's mother who lay lifeless on the road. The sailors were scrambling up the hill and the stairs in her direction. There wasn't enough time for Kayda to save them both, and humans weren't allowed in the Below.

The deepest part of the canal was under the bridge, and Kayda dove into it with the baby tightly tucked next to her. She maneuvered the underground cavern with ease until an opening on the right led her to a tunnel that would bring her to one of the many entrances to the Below. She swam through the underwater air pocket until she reached the metal gate.

Cyrus had the night shift, and she sighed in relief. He was more understanding than most. His hoofs clacked on the small walkway near the backdoor of the Below Administration and echoed off the domed brick walls of the tunnel between the entrances to the Below and the Above. He pulled on the rope from the pulley system on the wall, and the gate opened.

Kayda swam through just enough to allow him to close it behind her. She watched it drop down with sadness. That gate blocked her freedom.

"What are you doing here, Kayda?" he asked very much surprised to see her.

She carefully unfolded her wing to reveal the small babe she held tight to her body. The baby looked at her with kind, gentle eyes. It hadn't learned fear of creatures like her yet. It was the first time a human, albeit a hybrid one, didn't cower in terror when face to face with her.

"Ah," he said. "What have you got there?" He reached forward and took the baby. He held the little boy in front of him and remarked on how handsome the little fellow was. Cyrus was still smiling when he looked back at Kayda, but quickly noticed her downtrodden expression.

Cyrus looked from her to the tunnel from which she arrived and back again. "Perhaps you should stay for a bit, huh?" he asked.

Kayda looked in the direction she had entered mournfully. She hoped she would soon be reunited with her family. Turning back to Cyrus, she nodded.

The faun walked over to open the gate on the other side, and Kayda swam through into the Below. When the gate closed behind her, Cyrus cradled the baby in his arms and entered the back door of the Below Authority.

Ooh's and aah's erupted all around him as the workers took notice of the baby. "I think he shall be called Phillipe," Cyrus announced to the room. The door slowly closed behind him while a record keeper changed the paper on the wall. It had now been zero days since there had been an incident in the Above.

Chapter Four

Phillipe

Phillipe opened his eyes and looked up toward the ceiling. He'd had the nightmare again. It wasn't based on an actual memory. He would've been too young to remember anything. It was constructed from what he pictured happened to his parents from the details he'd been given as a young man. His parents were murdered when they tried to flee to safety. In the nightmare, they were always faceless shapes. His mind could add faces to the crew of the boat who killed them, but couldn't create a face for either of the two people he missed the most even though he never even met them.

He concentrated on the ceiling until the rounded shape of the light fixture started to come into focus. He had only ever known darkness. The Below did a good job of illuminating their world during daytime hours, but the lights went on and off like clockwork. At eight in the morning, one of the Below city workers would flip the switch, and it would appear as day until the switch was flipped off at eight in the evening. Twelve hours of night and twelve hours of light in a darkened world.

There were books filled with descriptions of sunrises and sunsets. Just once he'd love to feel the warmth of the sun on his skin or hear the call of a rooster waking the farm. It would never come to pass. A life Above was not his fate.

The internal clock ticking in his mind told him it was time to get up. He glanced at his alarm. The red digits on the screen read 6:28. He still had two minutes. He closed his eyes. Even the nightmares that haunted his dreams were better than his waking life. His eyes flew open again. *And today is Friday,'* he thought.

He groaned, sitting up and pushed the button to turn off the alarm. Fridays were the worst. Yanking his blanket off him, he climbed out of bed. Walking to the front door for his delivery, he flipped on every light as he passed blatantly ignoring the energy conservation warnings the Below had been issuing for years. He did his part. No one conserved water better than he did.

On the front stoop in a wire milk basket was a thirty-two ounce glass jar filled halfway with water. He glanced across the road at the other houses on his street. Their baskets were filled with bottles of milk and juice. He sighed and picked up his weekday morning ration. There would be more at work.

He shut the door and carried the bottle with him to the bathroom and set it on the counter under the mirror. His bathroom was tiny consisting only of a small counter, mirror, and a toilet. No tub. No shower. No sink basin. They weren't necessary.

The reflection in the mirror always seemed to look more defeated than he felt. It never ceased to amaze him how that was possible.

He unscrewed the top of the bottle and dipped his toothbrush down inside to wet it. He brushed thoroughly using the water sparingly to rinse and spit into the bowl of the toilet. The frothy foam of the toothpaste bubbled in the bright blue water of the toilet bowl. If he could have one thing in the world, just one small comfort item, it would be a sink.

'It's the creation of habit,' the voice mimicked inside his head.

Habits would be an easy thing to understand if reaching the surface was a possibility. When they first used that line on him over a thousand years ago, he was young. His naivety accepted it, and he cheerfully agreed to limited water in his home because it meant he could live on his own. He gladly accepted daily portions delivered at intervals to minimize the fluctuations of his growth.

It was painfully obvious he would never reach the surface which made this whole routine abundantly unnecessary. As it was his height in the Below remained a constant several inches higher than it would be Above. The air down here was rich with moisture from the ground around them. The cells in his body absorbed that moisture at a much faster rate than any other creature in existence. If he was going to be forced to stay in this darkened reality for the rest of eternity, he should be able to live his life at the height he wished as opposed to barely reaching 4' 5" on a good day.

The only running water in his home was to the toilet, and he had to beg for that. He was the last one to have indoor plumbing installed, and it took decades after the rest of the homes and businesses had been converted before they finally gave in to his request. Even then, the stipulation was the water to it had to be piped in with a chemical that would not only keep his toilet bowl shiny and clean, but the toxins it held would poison him if he tried to use the water for drinking or bathing. Not that he would ever be able to bring himself to do it. The blue tint of the water in the bowl was a constant reminder of the control the Below Authority had over him.

He pulled a wet disposable cloth out of a plastic bin of hygienic wipes. They were baby wipes. It didn't matter how cute they packaged them, or what name they slapped on the label. They were still baby wipes. It was an added insult to his short stature that he was expected to bathe with them. Except for Saturdays. That was shower day.

It was the one day of the week he looked forward to because of it. When he stepped out of the supervised shower at 6' 2", it was the only time he felt like he was truly himself.

He finished with the wipes and combed dry shampoo through his hair then took the bottle into the kitchen for breakfast. He ate and dressed for work. Another day, same routine.

Prior to leaving, he forced himself to drink the rest of the water. He had never known thirst and could probably go days without drinking anything before his body felt even the slightest effects from dehydration. His daily deliveries were a part of their habit building techniques. If he didn't use them, he would lose them. The Below Authority monitored his height. If he didn't consume the liquid they allowed him, they would decrease the amount delivered out of fear he was stockpiling it for some nefarious purpose.

Phillipe secured his briefcase in the basket on the back of his bicycle and rode the eight blocks to the Below Authority building where he parked it in one of the many racks amongst all the other workers. Many of them were arriving and greeting each other with their happy exclamations of, "TGIF!"

He avoided their cheerful small talk. He absolutely hated Fridays.

The Below Authority was the largest building in the city. It was a hundred yards long and two stories tall, not counting the many levels buried underground. He walked to the employee's entrance on the side and tried to pump himself up for the last day of a long work week.

He swiped his badge and heard the lock click. He pulled the door toward him and walked through, stepping to the side to catch his bearings. This hallway ran the full length of the building, and his office was the last one on the left.

Many times he had submitted a request to park on the other side of the building, the public parking side. The only employees allowed to park there were the ones in need of handicap access. He had tried, but his short legs didn't qualify him for it.

The hallway's ceiling was twenty foot high, and the walls were lined on either side with rows of frames that stemmed almost floor to ceiling. Here at the beginning they weren't pictures. They were simply lists of names. He began the long walk toward his office, keeping his eyes straight ahead.

'One, two, three,' he counted as he walked.

Long before the invention of photographs and before

paintings were done to document those who went Above...

'Ten, eleven, twelve.'

...the original Below Authority kept a list of names.

'Fourteen, fifteen, sixteen,' he paused. If he looked to the right two feet above his eye level, he would see the name Roark Jacoby, his father. His mother wasn't included on the wall. She had died bringing him into the world, but where the Below was concerned, she was nothing more than a mere human.

He quickened his pace after that. The list of names turned into drawings which turned into paintings that had been copied and shrunk down to fit a five by seven frame when technology permitted. Then there were the photographs, some candid and some posed.

In the beginning, there were mermaids, cyclops, and centurions. There were vast lands that hadn't been discovered or settled. These creatures could find a home Above and live undisturbed. As he neared his office, most of the faces staring at him appeared human. There were vampires and demigods with a smattering of a few other creatures. Almost anyone who can't pass as human weren't allowed into the Above anymore. There were a few exceptions such as the pixies. That was only because the Below didn't want them either.

Through the open doorway of his office, he saw the six files setting on his desk. Six individual pre-review meetings today. It was a loathsome workload for the end of the week.

He flipped the second switch turning on the remaining lights in the room. Setting his briefcase on the chair, he removed his jacket to hang on the rack in the corner. On the right side of his desk on a plain coaster was a mug containing eight ounces of coffee. It was covered with a decorative paper lid.

Phillipe flicked the lid off the mug and watched it fly over the edge of the desk. He carried it several doors down to the north side break room and popped it in the microwave to heat it up. Nothing made him feel like a child more than having an adult who was probably centuries younger than him measure out and deliver his drinks during the day.

Back in his office, he stored the files in a desk drawer for confidentiality save for his first appointment and the drink order that lay on top of the pile. The forty ounces of water he received daily, divided between the morning and evening, were fixed. He received three drinks of his choice a day, eight ounces each. Every Friday, he had to fill out the order that would begin on Monday of the following week. It included his choices for the weekends because the Below Authority was in control of his allotments and deliveries.

These things were done for a reason. It had made sense when it was first explained to him lifetimes ago, and he agreed to it. Back then, it never occurred to him how unlikely it would be that he could correctly guess whether he'd be in the mood for milk or juice with his lunch on Wednesday when filling out the order the Friday before.

He ticked the box for coffee in the morning every day of the week, and then made the rest of his choices at random. He'd have just as much luck making the selections blindfolded as he would trying to predict the future. The paper went into the outgoing tray on his desk. The drink order was the sole purpose of having an outgoing mail pickup in his office.

The first appointment of the day was in less than half an hour. He opened the file to see what to expect. One Lily Faestorm was scheduled in front of the review board next week and would be the first of the day to prepare for the meeting. *'A pixie,'* he sighed. The review wasn't necessary, but it was required. They were always sent straight to the surface.

Chapter Five

Invisibility

John Reed was his last appointment of the day, and Phillipe was ready to get the week over with. So far he'd seen a pixie which was really a drain on company payroll. If a pixie wanted to go to the Above once they had matured, they were sent to the head of the line. It was a needless waste of time for them to sit through a prescreening.

His next four appointments didn't want to go to the Above. Those were the ones he dreaded the most. It was decreed that each creature became eligible for review when they matured because the age of adulthood varied by species. If they were denied, the case would be reviewed again every ten years until they finally rose above the surface, or until they died. Some species, like the pixies, didn't have that long of a life span. Some species, unlike the pixies, were never granted access by the board. Yet they were still forced to go through the entire horse and pony show.

He felt for those species like the cyclops and the dragons who hadn't been allowed Above since explorers discovered more and more new areas, preventing them from having anywhere to live in secrecy. They were like him. Every ten years, their lives were disrupted, and they had to go to the meetings and sit before the review board even though the denial was a guarantee. They were like him except they were denied for different reasons.

It was the ones who were content where they were he didn't understand. It was beyond him why anyone would choose this way of life. It was dark, damp, and musty, and they were all confined to this one city. It was rather sizable, and they did expand as the population grew. It was still one place: the Below.

At least on the surface there was travel. There was no end to the places to visit and the new sights to see. There were palm trees and mountains. They could sunbathe on the shore of a lake. There was freedom.

The requirements were that the Below creatures had to blend in and couldn't reveal their true identity to anyone. Yes, the Above Guard did keep tabs on them and checked in on them from time to time to make sure everyone was keeping in line. There was still freedom.

The Below Security would no longer be watching their every move on the thousands of surveillance cameras positioned throughout the city. They weren't pulling you into the Authority offices to interrogate them when they took a different route home from work. It wasn't that much of an exaggeration. The Below liked stability and order. They depended on it to keep the city operating smoothly.

These creatures who walked into his office and announced they had no desire to leave angered him. Most of them would easily be granted access, but they turned up their nose at the opportunity that he so desperately craved. A knock on the open door interrupted his thoughts, and he looked up to see John Reed, a strange creature indeed.

"Come in," Phillipe said, standing from his seat and extending a hand toward the empty chair across the desk.

John glanced nervously down the hallway, "Uh, no, that's alright. This won't take long. I don't think."

'Another one,' Phillipe thought. *'One more content with being a bottom dweller.'*

"Actually these meetings tend to take the better part of an hour," Phillipe said, returning to his seat.

"Oh, well, um I thought I could just, uh," John stammered.

"You thought you could say you didn't want to go to the Above, and that would be it," Phillipe finished for him.

"Yeah," John said, stepping into the office. "I thought I had a choice."

"And you do," Phillipe agreed. "Once you get before the review board next week, they will ask you if it is your desire to live in the Above. This screening, however, is mandatory." Phillipe extended his hand to the chair again, giving John a nod indicating he might want to take a seat.

This time John complied and reluctantly pulled out the chair to sit.

"It is my job," Phillipe said, opening the file on his desk, "to make sure you have been informed of the process, you are aware of what to expect, and you feel prepared and confident to go in front of the review board."

"Yeah, but people like me never leave the Below," John told him.

Phillipe slowly skimmed through several pages of the file fully aware that John was fidgeting in his seat. It didn't bother him that John thought this was a waste of his time. Having people like John sit across from him was a waste of Phillipe's time.

More than that, it was a drain on his mental state that these people who had an opportunity to escape this dump would voluntarily choose to stay and continue to live in this hell. They could just as easily take a chance with the board where they might receive the green stamp of approval to live a life filled with possibility Above. Even if the board did reject them, there was always the appeal to the Chairman. It was rare, but he did sometimes approve select cases.

A second denial meant they would be trapped here another decade until their chance rolled around again, but at least they tried. He could respect the ones who made the endeavor even against all odds. They were like him. They yearned for independence and freedom, but were forced down here toiling under the control of the Authority living a vague resemblance of a life.

Satisfied with what he saw in the file, Phillipe clasped his hands together on top of the pages. Looking John in the eye, he asked, "People like you? With the power of invisibility, you mean?"

"Yes, exactly," John answered. "We're too much of a risk. Too likely to cause trouble."

"Ah, but that's where you're wrong," Phillipe corrected. "Just because no one of your kind has gone to the Above yet doesn't mean they never will. Let's begin, shall we?"

Phillipe pulled a prepared folder from his desk drawer

that contained a checklist of everything he was to cover in the meeting. It also contained several informational documents and pamphlets he had to pass along.

"The Below Authority and You" was written in gold letters in a circle around the Below's official seal on the front of the folder.

'*The Below Authority Against You. The Below Authority Controls You.*' There were so many more accurate wordings that could be used. It became harder and harder for Phillipe to hide his disgust each time he saw the words.

Phillipe began his spiel about the review process and what to expect knowing John didn't need to hear it. The local governing processes of the Below Authority, including the review board, was included in a required government class every year beginning in grade eight. By the time the students graduated at the end of grade twelve, every law, every ordinance of the Below had been so indoctrinated in their minds, they could recite them in their sleep. Yet every ten years starting at the age of maturity, the Below citizens had to sit in front of a screener and listen to it all again.

It had been over three hundred years since he transferred into this position. Some citizens he never saw a second time. Some he met with every decade right up until their last review before death. His bitterness had distorted and grew until it was a monster that was a separate entity from himself. It could talk to him from across the room, speaking aloud the thoughts in his head. Only Phillipe could hear its voice.

Maybe it was time for a change. He had considered it, but this job was cushy. It was easy and required very little effort on his part. Plus there were a few times when he truly did some good. It was rare, and he could count on one hand how many times it had happened. Occasionally, there was someone he actually helped. He hoped John Reed would be one of those cases.

After finishing the boring part, Phillipe said, "This is for you to take home and review," handing John the folder. "Or you can toss it straight into the recycle bin. It's up to you," he said honestly.

John laughed taking the folder and sliding it in front of him.

"Now, let's review your case." He flipped through a couple pages of John's file again. "I have to disagree with you John. I think you stand a very good chance of going to the Above," Phillipe said. "If that's what you want," he added.

"Well, yeah," John said. "I mean who doesn't want to go to the Above."

"You'd be surprised," Phillipe said shortly.

"It's just I've been told all my life I'll never be able to reach the surface because I can become invisible at will."

Phillipe nodded and exhaled slowly. John was right, partly. Since the Authority was officially established and procedures for relocating to the Above were put into place, no one with his power had been able to leave. They also had a tendency to disqualify themselves.

"The board consists of five Authority Council members. You need a vote of three in favor. Miller always votes no. He's old school. He's been on the board for forty-three years. It's time for him to retire. There has never been a single case where Miller has voted yes, not even for the pixies."

John laughed. If he thought Phillipe was joking, he was

wrong.

"Then there's Winger, and well, we'll call her Mrs. B. No one can pronounce her last name correctly. They vote solely based on the disciplinary record. John, what sets you apart from others of your kind is you have never been in trouble, not even a single detention while you were in school. You have never used your invisibility to cause mischief. You will get their votes. I'm certain of it."

"That's what held others back. It was too much of a risk they'd use their powers Above when they weren't under constant scrutiny. Whether they might do something childish like sneaking into a girls' locker room or something more criminal like committing theft, the board had concerns. You've kept your nose clean which alleviates that worry."

"Rockholm is a toss-up. She has been in that position for almost five years. Her votes are so random I've come to the conclusion she must be flipping a coin under the table. Birds, you go to the surface. Fish, you lurk below. Its luck, but you could get your third vote from her."

John played with the folder lining the spine straight against the edge of the desk. "So it's down to chance then?" he asked quietly.

"Not necessarily. The key is Masterson. He's the director of the Below Security. You need to appeal to his sense of law and order."

"But how?" John asked.

"You're a baker?"

"That's right," John nodded.

"One of the questions the review board will ask is how

can you add to the Above? What is it that you can bring that will contribute to their society, improve upon it, instead of just dwelling in it? I'll be honest with you being a baker doesn't cut it."

"Yeah," John nodded, looking down disappointed.

Phillipe knew he had him. John had started to like the idea of going to the surface. He had begun to believe it was possible, but Phillipe had just popped that bubble of hope.

"It says in your file you applied for a Below Security position when you graduated."

"That's right. I did, but in the physical, they discovered I had a heart murmur. It disqualified me."

Masterson hated the restrictions on Security applicants. He knew most of the medical conditions that disqualified them never affected anyone's ability to do their job. "Use that John."

"It's not in your file, but I remember a story about a boy with invisibility who had aided the Below Security in apprehended a burglar. Was that you?"

John inhaled deeply. "It was what made me want to join them. They placed me in the Cyclops' clock shop every night for almost a week because they felt it was the next likely target."

Phillipe grinned quietly. This was it. "When they ask you that question, admit it. Tell them being a baker wouldn't add anything that couldn't be found at any of the other existing bakeries. Tell them your dream was to join the Below Security. Remind them of how you helped catch a thief when you were a teenager. Say your hope is that your powers might be able to assist the Above Guard someday."

"And that will work?" John asked. "I'll be allowed to go to the surface."

Phillipe slowly nodded, then said, "No. I can't guarantee it, but I will tell you this. If that doesn't work, then I will admit you were right. No one of your kind will ever leave the Below."

Chapter Six

Escape

To say the light was blinding would be a gross miscalculation. It did render him unable to see with large dark spots left muddling his vision even with his eyes closed. It also burned like nothing he had ever felt before.

It was a little after three in the morning. Of the handful of times throughout the day he could make his move, this had been the one seemingly most advantageous. Not only was the Below Security away from this particular tunnel then, but most of the citizens were soundly tucked in bed. Or at least they had been until a few seconds ago.

The moment he opened the hatch to enter the sawing floor of the old windmill the alarm sounded in the Below. The noise barely reached his ears through the mile if not more of tunnel he had climbed through, but it was there. If he had looked down, he would've been able to make out the flashing red light near the tunnel entrance. Those lights were also illuminating the entire city. No one could sleep through it.

Phillipe had been brutally woken up to it himself on

many occasions. Everyone found their way outside to the darkened city streets. Partly to show they were accounted for and not the one who dared try to escape. Mostly out of curiosity to see which of their friends or neighbors had committed the ultimate crime. None of the attempts in his lifetime had ever made it to the surface. That was until now.

After making it through the hatch, the alarms activated immediately because he didn't have clearance. They would be behind him in the tunnel already. He opened the door to leave the windmill as soon as he spied it and was hit with the overwhelming brightness of the sun.

'*Well played,*' he thought. In the months he spent planning, he never came across anything saying the Above and the Below were on opposite schedules. It was a genius tactic. Escapes would be virtually impossible to attempt during the day underground. Security teams were everywhere. All escapees had ventured to reach freedom under the cover of night, same as Phillipe. If anyone managed to make it to the surface, they wouldn't have the cover of darkness to hide them, and they would be faced with having to adjust their eyes. All the while the Above Guard would be bearing down upon them.

He couldn't hesitate any longer. Opening the door again, he shielded the sun from his eyes with his hand and squinted his eyes till they were almost shut. He jumped off the edge of the platform instead of using the stairs and ran toward the trees with his eyes closed. He stumbled several times and fell twice.

Once in the shadows of the woods, he tried to open his eyes, but the light breaking through the branches was still too bright. Citizens who made the vertical move were acclimated. It was a long process, and Phillipe didn't know what all it entailed.

The Below Security would be on the surface any second. This was turning into a nightmare. He had made it farther than any other escapee, but that wouldn't matter if he got caught before he accomplished what he was here to do. It was supposed to be the middle of the night when he arrived, making it easier for him to remain undetected.

He ran through the woods to the river that flowed nearby. His original plan was to hike the banks until he reached the city then take a dip in the water to transform. Staying small would help him in a chase. He wouldn't be able to outrun the Security with his shorter legs, but his size would help him hide and maneuver through places they wouldn't be able to fit.

Thinking he'd have the night to hide him, he escaped in his Saturday clothes. Less to carry with him, and he'd have something that would fit when his size grew. Now, they were a hindrance as he tried to run without being able to see while holding his clothes up off the ground to avoid tripping.

It was chaos. The plan needed to be reshaped only he didn't have the luxury of the time needed to do it. He'd have to wing it which allowed for limitless errors that couldn't be foreseen.

Once he reached the river, he jumped in the water. It had been his plan all along to enter the city at his tallest form. Someone at his Below height, a dwarf as they were called, would be noticed. He'd stand out in a crowd easily, making it painless for the Guard to find him. That wasn't the only reason. Almost no one had ever seen him at his full form. Cameras weren't allowed in the showers, and the yearly picture they took of him for his file would be hard to use to identify him. He saw to that.

Phillipe hadn't planned to dunk himself out in the open. The dazzling array of lights shooting from his body were hard to see in the middle of the day. This far from the city he would be less likely to happen upon anyone who might take notice. Any risk, no matter how small, was extremely dangerous. When he gets caught which is inevitable, the punishment will be death. He could either risk causing a disturbance so soon, or risk the Guard finding him with unfinished business. He chose the former and floated down the river until it curved around the capital.

The river curved sharply to the left, and Phillipe knew he was entering the area where it wrapped around the city. The current was light, and he fought without difficulty to get to shore. The glowing lights that illuminated his presence stopped when he emerged from the river.

He sat upon a fallen tree to bask in the sun and tried to gauge how long it would take the Below Security to find him. They wouldn't have alerted the Above Guard this soon, and they certainly wouldn't dive into the river. He had a small window of time.

The clothes would dry quickly, much faster for him than anyone else as his body greedily absorbed every drop of moisture. In a few minutes, he began his trek into the city. The clothing was still damp, but it would dry before he arrived. He needed to drop in on an old friend before the alerts went out to all the creatures living in secrecy amongst the humans. His friend was a good man who owed him a favor. Good, but strange, very strange indeed.

Phillipe set out to make his way keeping to the woods for as long as possible. The closer he got to the city he would encounter people along the way. Country dwellers, hikers, and other exercise enthusiasts enjoyed the country roads. He wouldn't be able to identify those looking for him. The Guard would blend in with the residents of the area. The only people on the surface who knew of their existence were the creatures who came from the Below. Anyone could be searching for him, even his old friend John Reed. That was a risk he'd have to take.

Chapter Seven

The Favor

Phillipe reached the city and was lost. He had studied a map of the city, had committed his route to memory. Having to make some rash alterations to his plan caused him to not enter where he had intended. He walked around trying to get his bearings, trying to find even one street name that sounded familiar to him. He would walk in one direction for a few blocks then would worry he was going farther away from his destination and then walk back the way he came.

Virtually no one paid him any mind. They were busy with their own lives, jobs, errands and enjoying themselves. He looked essentially the same as they did maybe dressed a little differently. It was an odd thing being among them. The first human he passed by while holding his breath for fear of being outed never gave him a second glance. Then the next and the next walked right passed him as though he belonged.

His whole life he had been told it didn't matter what form he chose. As a dwarf, he'd be singled out. Human dwarves were already an object of ridicule. Plus his dwarf height would fluctuate based on the humidity in the air. Even as a regular sized man, he would stick out like a sore thumb. That's what the Authority told him.

Yet here he was walking down the street with them. He waited in a crowd for the cross walk light to signal it was safe. He began to garner the courage to wave hello to strangers, and no one suspected a thing.

Finally he found the street he was looking for, Franklin Avenue. He headed left since that was the side of the street he was on and looked at the number of the first business he passed, 1408. He continued on to the second shop, 1406. He was going in the right direction, but he was still seven blocks away.

Phillipe continued to walk at a fast pace toward the bakery he needed to find. His worry steadily grew that the alert had already been signaled. Each person he passed on the street was a possible Guard member, and he studied them secretly for any sign. They nodded their heads and smiled their hellos. His confidence grew, and he muttered his own greetings in return. For thirteen hundred years, he'd been told he would never fit in on the surface. Here he was nailing it on day one without the training and transition process required by the Authority.

Almost every stranger was kind and polite. There were a few who kept to themselves, staring intently at the sidewalk. Cars drove by, and some of the occupants waved as they went. They had no idea as they continued on with their day they were witness to a monster. He might appear as a man, but cruel intent was in his heart. These people had the clues, if they could only remember them later, which might assist detectives in catching a murderer.

The mouthwatering aromas from the All You Knead bakery would signal he was close even without the street numbers directing him. The closer he came the more adrenaline pumped through his veins. He was almost in the clear and not a moment too soon. He could feel the wetness dripping down his back which could only mean his rudimentary stitches had ripped. He was bleeding, but it would be alright soon. It would only be a few more steps, but at any moment, the Guard could appear causing him to have to figure out how to circumvent them.

Phillipe pushed the door open and stepped inside. A handful of customers were seated at tables in the small dining area off to the side. Some of them looked up to see who had entered, but the rest continued reading their newspapers or were deeply vested in conversation, not letting the distraction interrupt them.

"I'll be with you in a minute," a voice yelled from the back. It'd been too long for Phillipe to tell if he recognized it or not.

Two sides of the shop were lined with counters and glass cases of every imaginable delectable from breads to cookies to cakes and more he couldn't recognize. Sacks awaiting pickup lined the counter behind the glass cases with order forms stapled near the top. John had done well for himself.

He walked to the counter near the register and waited for the person who belonged to the voice to appear. If it was anyone else, he'd have to switch to Plan B which was little better than panic and hope he didn't get caught.

To great relief, it was John Reed who walked through

the swinging door that separated the store front from the kitchen. The corner of Phillipe's mouth pulled up tight. He would not be recognized at this height. It'd been five years since they last spoke. John wouldn't be able to recognize him at all after that length of time regardless of size if it weren't for the rarity of dwarfism.

"May I help you," John said with a smile, wiping his hands on a small towel that hung from the belt of his apron.

"You're the only one who can," Phillipe told him.

John's eyes squinted at the unusual response. "What can I do for you?"

"I believe you owe me a favor."

"I'm sorry. I don't know what this is about. If there is anything I can get for you..." John's voice trailed off, and he fidgeted nervously.

Phillipe nodded and leaned in closer. He lowered his voice in case any nosy patrons were minding someone's business other than their own. "It's been five years. You probably forgot about our pre-screening meeting where you learned exactly how to make this vertical move."

His expression remained blank for several seconds then the realization showed behind his eyes. "But... You're..."

"Yes," Phillipe said glancing down his body to his feet. "I look a little different than you remember."

A smile broke wide across John's face. "That's great. When did you get to town?"

'How sweet,' Phillipe thought. *'He thinks they'd actually let me leave.'*

"Just this morning," Phillipe told him.

John busied himself grabbing a box and filling it with an

assortment of pastries.

"About that favor," Phillipe reminded him.

"Consider it a welcome gift," John said, setting the box between them. "Do you drink coffee?" he asked, picking up a cup without waiting for an answer. "How do you take it?"

"No, John," Phillipe said. "John!" He repeated louder when it became obvious John wasn't going to stop adding to the care package he was making.

John stopped mid-stride and turned to look at him.

"The favor," Phillipe repeated again. His irritation was growing, and he tried to convey it without speaking too loud.

"That's right," John said coming back toward Phillipe. "Anything you need. What can I help you with?"

"I need a place to stay for a few days."

John was an open book. The thoughts that fired rapidly through his mind could be read effortlessly in his expressions over the next several seconds. He went from being willing to eagerly offer Phillipe a place to crash, to curiosity about why he may be in need, to ultimately the stark realization that something was amiss. The Guard would never let a creature from the Below stray too far. If something happened, anything at all, they would become involved.

A creature who couldn't cut it in the human world would be sent back. There could be zero risk to their world being discovered, and all it would take was one rogue outcast drawing attention to himself. If they couldn't maintain stable employment, couldn't pay their rent or mortgage, they would receive a one way ticket to the Authority office. Even creatures at odds with their significant other would be swiftly moved to a new location by order of the Authority. It would be impossible for Phillipe to need a place to stay without the Guard taking part in arrangements.

Before John could form his questions into words, a series of chimes rang out through the bakery. One by one, customers viewed the notification on their phones. John pulled his phone from his apron pocket and slowly lifted his eyes to Phillipe after looking at the screen.

Phillipe strained his neck to see for himself, and John turned the phone toward him. It was an emergency alert about an escaped prisoner named Phillipe Jacoby, using the only photo the Authority had on file for him. Not only was it outdated, but it was his shortened form as well.

'Very well played,' he thought. By labeling it a prison break, all citizens of the Above would be on the lookout, not just the ones who hid in the open. He smiled, pleased with the effort he put into his escape. He could've taken all the pictures from his file, but there was something sporty about leaving them a breadcrumb to follow.

"What have you drug me into?" John asked.

Chapter Eight

The Alarm

It was almost half past three when the silent alarm triggered in the private office Liam shared with his partner Adam, who was in a meeting with new recruits. It was a consulting office that mysteriously never took on new clients. Business was booming for appearances sake, but it was one of many fronts for the Guard. A banner dropped over the web page he was viewing with the details of the escapee, and he could hear the vibration of the alarm in the back room. Without reading the information, he walked back to silence it. Once the alarm was initiated by the Below, he had a short two and a half minute window to deactivate it before everyone under his watch, Guard and citizens alike, received an emergency notification.

As Chief of the Guard, protocol called for him to immediately send the nearest agents to where the escapee attempted to flee, but he didn't see the rush. No one had ever made it to the surface before regardless of the route they chose to escape. The closest was long before Liam's time when a gnome hitched a ride in the luggage of someone making the transition to the Above. It was one of a thousand reasons why newcomers' possessions were thoroughly searched. While the gnome had technically made it to the surface, he never made it out of the containment room, never had the pleasure of a breath of fresh air.

Instead of sending his agents out on a wild goose chase through the countryside near Rotterdam, he would wait it out as he always had and file fake paperwork at the end of his shift. There was no need in riling up the guards and creating senseless gossip that would spread like wildfire through the creatures they protected. They needed to believe the safety of the system worked in order for them to maintain control. It wouldn't take more than a suggestion that someone could overcome it, and they would descend into chaos.

Back at his desk, he read the information sent to him by the Below Security. There was no picture attached which didn't stay true to code. The weight and height weren't fixed either, but rather a range. The numbers filled in those lines were a significantly broad span. It was becoming increasingly odd, and Liam was ready to chalk it up to a kink in the system. This warning had to be a mistake, and any minute the Below would contact him with their weak apologies and poor explanations. As he turned his head, he saw it. There was one small detail he hadn't taken into consideration, creature race.

"A hydrohomunculus?" Liam pondered out loud. It would explain the height and weight listed. He could be any size really. The picture wasn't nearly as necessary with this added bit of information. There was only one. It could only be Phillipe. Most of the Above would recognize him on sight as they had to pass through his office on their way to the surface until a few years ago when he switched departments. Shoot, most of the creatures up here credited Phillipe as the reason why they were granted the approval.

That could be the reason they didn't include the photo. Annual pictures were taken, but it was anyone's guess up here if they kept one of each height extreme in Phillipe's file. It would be the smart choice, but that may turn into a hindsight being twenty-twenty issue. Assuming, of course, he escaped at his full size.

It almost didn't seem possible. A lot of the tunnels were small, and the Security members that fit through them were petite and below average height. At his full size, there were very few routes Phillipe could take and none would lead him to Rotterdam, not without days of traveling after arriving up top.

Liam leaned back hooking his elbow over the edge of the chair really considering the possibilities now. It was like a puzzle, and his mind was determined to solve it. The tunnels were rigged with various access points where Security members had to swipe their badge or enter their code to be allowed to enter. Escapees would activate the alarm at these points, or the alarm could've been activated by someone in the Below who had clued in on the escapee's intentions.

He thought about the nearest entrance point to Rotterdam. It would have to be the old windmill. *'That tunnel is so narrow,'* he thought. Phillipe would only make it through in his dwarf size, the size the Below insisted on keeping him.

It would make more sense for him to flee at his full

height. Phillipe's strides would be longer. He'd cover more ground faster, and no one would recognize him. There was only one person who ever saw him in that form, and that was the Security member assigned to him during his showers.

'Patrick!' Liam thought, sitting upright so fast his swivel chair almost bounced him to the floor.

Patrick had just passed away three days ago of a sudden heart attack. It left no living person with a recollection of Phillipe at his full height. The funeral was to be held today in the Below. Their opposite schedule meant their day wouldn't begin for almost five hours. Liam had granted many of his Guard to have the day off to rest to attend the services later.

The lack of picture signaled they didn't have one of him at his full height to share for one reason or another. Phillipe couldn't have planned this better. Either that or he fell into an opportunity and chose to take advantage of it. However, Liam was already growing suspicious into whether investigations into Patrick's death were necessary.

There was one way left to find him; his tracker. Liam's fingers flew across the keyboard. He copied Phillipe's identification number and entered it into the security software. When he accessed the tracker information, it showed Phillipe was safe at home, probably in bed as it was the middle of the night there.

It couldn't be right. The Below would have checked his home and would have checked his tracker location by now.

'Unless he cut it out.' The thought made Liam cringe, and he wasn't sure it was possible without help. Trackers were placed below the shoulder blade in the back on the right side. Liam stretched his arms over and around his body,

but he couldn't reach the location where trackers were implanted. He shivered, thankful neither the Guard nor Security detail had to wear one. Phillipe had to have someone help him.

He had to be in his dwarf form which meant he had to intend on transforming soon after reaching the surface. *'The river,'* Liam thought, jumping to his feet. He grabbed his phone thinking off the top of his head which team was closest to that side of the city to send into the woods for a search. He'd regret this delay for the rest of his life. Valuable minutes were lost because he felt complacent in believing their systems would prevent an actual threat like this.

Mags and Pershall had the sixth district patrol. They'd be able to take a drive to the windmill easily enough. Before Liam could call them, his phone rang in his hands. It was Masterson looking for an update he couldn't give. He swiped to send the call to voice mail. His job was as good as over after this, but he wouldn't let that happen until he had a chance to make it right.

Chapter Nine

The Disappearance

The constant shrill of the siren was deafening in Gordy's ears. Crews were in place as soon as the door to the windmill had been opened. It would still be several hours before anyone learned how Jacoby managed to make it through two security checkpoints in the tunnel without triggering an alarm.

His boss Masterson wouldn't reset the alarm and blinding red lights. Some flashed bright enough to create residual spots in his vision that made it just as difficult to see during the pauses, and others beamed constantly shining their light circularly around where they were positioned. Spotlights of blinding white scoured throughout the city. Worst of all, the shrill repetitive blaring of the alarm echoed inside his ears, bounced off his ear drums, and was beginning to cause physical pain.

As soon as the door was opened, security cameras revealed who it was in the windmill. The employee on shift at the base of the tunnel was taken into questioning. A flurry of activity was everywhere as teams searched every inch of the Below. Some were on surveillance video, teams were headed up the tunnel in hot pursuit, and others like him were given various other tasks to investigate.

Gordy and his partner had just arrived inside of Jacoby's home to rifle for evidence. On their way, they received a call telling them Jacoby would be home. Something didn't sit right. Either they misidentified the suspect opening the door of the windmill, or they tracking system was defunct. Even if it had been missed that he did re-enter the windmill, there was no way Jacoby could've decided against the escape and make it back home in this short amount of time. Not to mention making his way past the army of Security scouring the Below.

One theory is that Jacoby didn't escape at all. He was a patsy used by the real culprit to throw everyone off track. He'd been down here almost longer than anyone. It wasn't likely for him to try to make a run for it now after all this time. The second time he opened the windmill door a ray of light glared across the cameras, and who left the windmill couldn't be seen.

It'd be practically improbable for him to make it back home before Security teams swarmed the tunnel. There were plenty of off shoots that could lead him almost anywhere in the Below if someone informed him of where to go. More likely, he was hiding in the windmill, waiting for the right moment to return.

Starting at the back of the house, they went systematically room by room leaving nothing unsearched. He was in the bedroom tearing apart the bed and readying to empty the dresser when his partner called for him. He went out in the hallway and saw an open door with light shining from inside. As he approached, he could see the look on his partner's face. It was a mixture of being stunned, shocked and absolute terror.

"What is it?" Gordy asked.

His partner didn't answer.

Gordy followed his gaze to the counter below the mirror in the bathroom. Floating in a bottle of pink tinted water was the encapsulated tracking chip. Pieces of flesh still clung to it.

It was his turn to be captivated by it. He picked up the bottle, holding it inches from his face and peered closer. It was impossible for him to have done this on his own. They would be expanding their search for an accomplice. Someone else had to cut this out of Jacoby's back.

He was so fixated on the bottle he barely noticed his partner had finally regained his wits and was calling in to base that Jacoby wasn't there. Their boss's voice was hardly discernable as his thoughts stayed with the chilling sight in the glass bottle. He also didn't notice the decrease in noise outside. The alarm had been turned off. Jacoby wasn't in the Below.

Gordy looked around, but the room was clean. Not a single drop of blood anywhere. It might not have happened here. He carried the bottle out of the bathroom following the sound of his partner's voice. His partner was animated like he was yelling at him to hurry, but the sound met his ears as a distorted, echoing whisper.

As they passed the kitchen on their way out of the house, something caught the corner of his eye. It was out of place and seemed unusual to him, but he couldn't quite understand. His mind wasn't able to keep up with translating the images from his eyes. Then it hit him.

Everything flooded in at once. The lack of alarm and flashing lights outside the windows was clear. There was nothing but darkness beyond these walls. His partner's voice practically screamed at him, "Gordy!" But he stayed fixated on the spot where the refrigerator met the kitchen cabinets. "Snap out of it! We got to go," he yelled, as he inched backward to the door.

"Look," Gordy said softly and pointed. He walked across the kitchen until he was several inches from the blade then turned sideways and compared the height with his own. The knife was wedged in tight and came almost to Gordy's waist. For a man like Jacoby, it would be perfect.

There were dried droplets on the floor under the blade. If there had been anything more, it had since be cleaned. *'The entire house was meticulously tidy,'* Gordy thought. "He wouldn't be able to stand the mess in the kitchen this had to create, but he wanted us to know he was working alone," he told his partner.

"The crazy fool cut it out himself. I don't know how he managed it, but he did," Gordy thought out loud.

"We've got to get back to headquarters," his partner urged.

Gordy glanced in his direction not really seeing him. The blood had drained from his face, and he was as pale as a sheet. He radioed his commander as if on autopilot and would have no recollection of doing it later.

The radio crackled as the commander's voice came back

across the air waves. "Tell me you have Jacoby! That you made a mistake. We need answers about who he's working with. We need to know exactly who we're searching for on the surface." Masterson barked.

This was the one part of the job he hated. The concept of don't shoot the messenger always seemed to get lost during stressful times.

Gordy squeezed his eyes shut and rubbed his temple, holding the radio near his mouth. "No, sir. He's not here. There's evidence to suggest he cut his implant out."

There was silence over the radio, and Gordy knew Masterson's office was being turned upside down as his commander threw everything he could lift in a fit of rage. "New orders," the voice on the radio announced. "Head over to Peterson's place. See what you can find."

"Do you really think he's there?" Gordy asked.

"No," Masterson replied. "I think they're frolicking through a meadow, side by side, holding hands. Get over there!" Over the loud, irate voice of his boss, Gordy could still detect the cracking sound Masterson's knuckles made as he clenched and unclenched his fists repeatedly.

Gordy looked at his partner and nodded. They headed out the door on their way to the home of the Security team member who was supposed to be on duty at the tunnel entrance that evening.

Chapter Ten

Changes

It had been a little over three months since Phillipe transferred departments, and not a day went by when he didn't regret it. His old position had been easy. Boring, yes. Repetitious, definitely. There was little to it, and the pay was good. The thing that bothered him the most about it was helping people see a world he could never see, or sitting by and listening to them explain why they didn't care to see it. Anyone who wouldn't take advantage of the opportunity to leave this underground dungeon existence was making a ridiculous mistake in his opinion.

When he applied for research and tracking, he thought he'd be monitoring the tracking devices of the Below citizens, performing maintenance on the system, updating their software. It was how the position was advertised.

During the interview, no one told him any different. When they offered him the job, it was a completely different role. He found out they were excited to have him come on board because of his extensive knowledge of those Above. One of their employees would be retiring soon, and they wanted to go ahead and bring him in to train.

It was a different area of research and tracking. He'd be preparing profiles for those who went Above to help the Above Guard understand what to expect from the newcomers. In addition, he'd have a caseload of creatures to monitor. Phillipe would have to keep an eye on their every move as part of an early detection program to see if anything looked awry.

Part of him never understood why he took the job. He had wanted to get away from being reminded daily of what he was missing. This was a more in depth excursion into what he could never have. Perhaps that's why he did it, to live vicariously through those who were lucky enough to bask in the sun without tolerating those who had no desire to ever feel it on their skin. It only served to grow his bitterness against those who kept him in the darkness.

One of his first caseloads was Meredith Jennings. Her parents had passed when she was a toddler. It was a car wreck that left her orphaned. Had they lived, she'd never have suffered a day in the Below unless there was cause to remove her. Creatures born above were allowed to stay and were brought up never knowing the unending torture of living in the ground.

There was a lot to be said about the lengths the Authority went to in trying to make it bearable. Fresh air was piped in from various access points above ground. Children would find the access pipes and clog them with litter or dirt, or worse. The uses they found for the pipes were obscene. Any blockages would be cleared, and the pipes would be cleansed. Even having one pipe down made a terrible difference in air quality.

Progress brought along the invention of air filter systems, and that made a huge difference all around. The pipes were still in use, but they were no longer at the mercy of young punks goofing off. Buildings and homes were constructed well. The air flow inside never served as a reminder of how far below ground they actually were.

There were no motorized vehicles in the Below. All transportation was by foot or bicycle. Most of the comforts were here. Streams and ponds were constructed to give the appearance of normal country sides. With recent developments in the infrastructure of television and radio, they now had their own channels. It was mostly all news and music, but it was more entertainment then they had in the past.

It was claustrophobic. The knowledge that you could ride around the entire perimeter of the Below in less than a day made everything feel smaller than it already looked. It was never the going anywhere new, meeting new people, or making new friends which drained even the most joyful among them.

Meredith was being given all those opportunities. With the tragic death of her parents, it was a certainty she'd be granted the chance to go back as long as there were no problems with her behavior that would warrant red flags. The review had already been done, and the approval granted.

She was acclimating now. It was a long process that included training in everything humans learned from birth like how to operate a microwave. There would be a slow exposure to the sun to get her used to the blinding light of the rays. The Above Guard would even teach her how to drive a car.

While she was in the process of learning everything Phillipe could only dream of doing, he was stuck miles below the surface creating her file. If her parents were alive, she would be assigned to the employee who oversaw them. The person who was their tracker fifteen years ago had since retired. Her parents' files were in the archives in one of the sub basements of the Authority. None of the information was kept in a computer database where it could be hacked.

Phillipe stared at his desk, not wanting to complete the work. The archives held all the files of every creature who had ever gone to the surface. The information on those who never left the Below were stored elsewhere. The room spanned almost the entire area of the Authority building with floor to ceiling files. There had to be records of millions of people that had made the move, but he was stuck here forever because he had been rebellious growing up as an orphan.

There was a significant pay increase with his new position, but money wasn't a driving force. It was only him, and he made more than enough. Most people saved to open a business which he had no desire to do. The other real need for money was to have a cushion when you, or your child, were granted approval to ascend. Neither of which he had to concern himself with because he never had children and would never be allowed to go above ground himself. He stared at the empty file on his desk, and the computer generated labels he still had to affix to it. For at least the twelfth time that day, he contemplated quitting.

Chapter Eleven

The Archives

The archives were four levels below the ground floor of the Authority building. Elevators were non-existent in the Below. It wasn't bad going down, but the hike back up took a toll on his short legs. This was the first time he had to venture down there since his orientation during the transfer to the new position.

He was brought down into the outer office and introduced to Maude who was essentially the glorified librarian of the records. She was a faun who first came to this department over a hundred years ago. It was a position Phillipe could've easily put in for when it became open if he'd had any interest in it. The Authority preferred immortals or those with extreme longevity working the records room.

During his tour, he hadn't actually gone past the outer office. His mentor only brought him to the windows that lined the back of the office, showing him the seemingly endless rows of files. Each row was sectioned multiple times as it extended with an identifier at the end labeling what names were contained within.

After meeting Maude, it was explained the process he'd go through for entrance, but once inside the record room, he was on his own. There were no other record keepers besides her, and she had more than enough work to keep her busy than to have to help any employee navigate the alphabet to find the name they needed.

Depending on the work he was doing, he could take the file to one of a number of tables scattered throughout the huge storage room to search for the information he needed. Otherwise, he could check the file out like a book for three days, and only three days. The repercussions for not returning it or all of the information stored inside it were severe.

There were no cameras in the archives. It would be too easy for hackers in the system to zoom in on any files that were being opened. That also meant if he fell from a ladder he could be there till the end of Maude's shift when she searched for stragglers, ordering them to leave.

It was an urban legend around the Below. An Authority employee fell in the archives room and bled to death waiting for someone to discover him or hear his cries, but help never came. No one really knew if it was true. Each person who told the story had their own variation of when it happened and who it was. No one except Phillipe. He was leaving work when they carried the poor creature out of the basement sublevels. He'd been dead for hours before being discovered.

Phillipe put his hand on the office door and pushed it open. The handset of the telephone was cradled beneath her chin and rested on her shoulder while her fingers flew across the keyboard. "Unh-huh," she said, turning to look at Phillipe. She held one finger to him, motioning for him to wait a minute. "Yeah, got it," she said, turning in her chair to face him. "Sounds good. Yeah, bye," she cradled the phone and narrowed her eyes at him.

"I wondered how long it'd be before you made your way down here." Maude held out her hand. "Paperwork?"

He handed her the form he'd printed that morning and had his supervisor sign.

Maude looked it over carefully. "Jennings. Oh," she lifted her eyes toward Phillipe. "Meredith is finally on her way? Sweet girl."

Phillipe swallowed his disgust. Sweet or not, she was going to the surface on a pity vote. "Yes. I need her parents' files in order to create hers."

She nodded. "Go on ahead," she said, jerking her head toward the archive door. "I'll hang onto this until you leave." She slid the paper across her desk and weighted it down with a stapler.

Inside the archives, he walked down the end of the rows, reading the labels until he found where he needed to go. There were multiple sections to each row, and the long lines of files went on in all directions once in the midst of them. It was like a maze that could easily turn you around until you were lost.

As he walked down the row, lights ahead of him went on automatically. Most things in the Below were motion activated. It was the Security office's way of reminding everyone they were always being watched.

Records went back to the creation of the Below. It wasn't

as old as time itself. There had been a long stretch after monkeys walked upright out of the jungle beginning the order of humans that exist today before any creatures had to go into hiding. Every creature that wasn't accepted as real in the human world, but had existed alongside people since the Below originated had a file in this room. The ones who never made it to the surface had their records kept in a closet two floors up.

He carefully scoured the signs along each column of file drawers, looking for Jennings' parents. At last he found the right area, and he drug a ladder down, positioning it next to where he needed it. It was on wheels and connected to the shelves similar to ladders in large libraries of bygone days on the surface. The drawer he needed was about halfway up. He rifled through it for the files on Meredith's parents and pulled them out, resting them on the other folders in the drawer. He didn't want to spend more time in the eerie room than necessary. There was a small notebook in his pocket, and he was pulling it out to jot down the information he was after when he saw it out of the corner of his eye.

The drawer to the left was labeled Ja-Jah. *Jacoby,*' he thought. *'My parents would be in there.'*

When he was finished with the Jennings files, he used the drawer handle to pull himself, and the ladder, over. He opened the drawer and quickly found their files. They were the only two Jacoby's in there, Esther and Roark. His father had changed his surname, but Phillipe was never told why.

The door to the archives opened, and another agent walked inside to do his own research. Phillipe's heart rate quickened, and he panicked. All of this information was considered highly confidential. It didn't matter that these were his parents. If he was caught snooping in a file without permission, he'd be terminated on the spot.

Without thinking his actions through, he hurriedly put the file folders back in the drawer and removed the Jennings' files. He would take them to his desk to do the research after his heart started beating normally again. Climbing off the ladder, he headed to the office as fast as his legs would carry him.

He walked through the door, and Maude turned to him. "Got what I needed," he said, holding up the files on Meredith's parents. "I'll have them back to you as soon as I can."

Phillipe only took a single step away from her desk when she stopped him. "Hold up," she ordered. "Let me see those."

The sound of his heart beat echoed in his ears as he handed the files to her. Phillipe wasn't sure how she knew what he'd been up to, but it was the only explanation. She reached under her desk, and he knew she was signaling Security to arrest him.

To his surprise, she opened a desk drawer and pulled out a small, handheld device. Maude checked the names on the files then opened each of them, scanning the top pages to make sure they matched. She turned the small machine on and pushed a button. A red light shone from the top, and she scanned it over the front of each file until it beeped. The place was different for both. It was near the middle of the file of Meredith's mother and in the bottom left for her father.

"No one puts it in the same place," she muttered, sounding frustrated. She looked up at Phillipe, waiting for something. "That's right. You're new. I need your badge."

Phillipe handed it to her, not sure what she was doing, but he was feeling more confident he wasn't about to have his life turned upside down for making the stupid mistake of giving in to temptation to see his parent's files. She scanned the electronic strip on the back of the badge and handed it back.

On the computer, Maude pulled up a screen and hit a few keys. "There. The files are checked out to you. You have exactly seventy two hours from now to return them, and you cannot remove them from the Authority building. I can't stress that enough. Don't take your work home with you."

"Got it," Phillipe nodded. He picked up the files off her desk and left the office. He took the stairs two at a time on his way up wanting to get back to the safety of his desk before his heart gave out. It was a wonder his little legs didn't trip, causing him to fall down a flight and bust his head open at the bottom.

He slumped into the chair behind his desk, clutching the files to his chest. Once he could breathe again without audibly hearing each intake of air, he laid them in front of him, side by side. Synchronizing his movements, he opened each file and closed them again repeatedly before finally stacking them one atop the other. He closed his eyes and leaned back in his chair, regretting every decision he had made in the last thirteen centuries that led to this moment.

Chapter Twelve

Buried Secrets

Phillipe stared at the files on his desk, the Jennings. He didn't need much information to prepare Meredith's file, and he had already jotted down those few details in his pocket notebook while he was in the archives. If he had simply done what he was supposed to in the records room, he would've missed out on the opportunity that had fallen into his lap.

The mother's file was on top, and he pushed it off and to the side. Mr. Jenning's file stared at him, beckoning him. He opened it and sat back hastily. His heart beat quickened again, and he glanced nervously around his office before his eyes settled on the door. There were no cameras in here, but the large window on the office door allowed all eyes to spy his way as they passed by. They wouldn't know. They couldn't know what he was doing.

It took several deep breaths and a lot of convincing himself that he was out of the woods to get his heart to stop pounding loud enough to ring in his ears. He tried to flip up the pages in the file. Several times he tried to order his hand to move, but it wouldn't obey the command.

'New tactic,' he thought.

Phillipe rearranged everything on his desk to pull Meredith's file closer. He began affixing the labels for her name and creature classification. On his computer, he logged into the rotary address software. It had a different name, but he preferred to call a spade a spade. Tracking creatures was the sole purpose of it.

The computer system only held the files of the living and only of those living on the surface. Once they passed away, the online file was deleted, and the paper one was stored away. Creatures like himself had hard files only. There wouldn't be a computer system at all if it didn't make it easier for the Above Guard to access the information for themselves. They had to fight for it too. The Authority is extremely careful about external breeches, but even more cautious about internal ones.

It was easy data entry work to fill out the fields for Meredith. He had all the pertinent information for her already, but a few details needed to be garnered from her parent's files which he did easily enough. His hands had no difficulty shuffling through their paperwork when it was necessary for his job.

The paperwork began printing, and Phillipe stared at the computer screen watching the print job progress bar slowly move to the right as the job came closer to completion. The file of Meredith's dad was calling to him. It was a small brown folder with snippets of a life lived stored inside. It was an inanimate object no more than nine by twelve inches, but it was the largest item in the office. Its presence overwhelmed him and sucked the air of the small confines of the room.

The printer quit spewing out documents, and he grabbed them, sliding them all into Meredith's file for confidentiality. They could be arranged later. Phillipe took her dad's file and reached for the loose papers in the back. He pulled them out, folded them in half, and then shoved them in the bottom of his briefcase he kept on the ledge behind his desk.

He wanted to head back to the archives, to return the files as quickly as possible. It would be risky. Maude might remember that one of the files had been significantly larger if he takes them back now. Plus, it would be an easy tell that he didn't have to check them out. If he only needed them less than an hour, then surely he should've been able to get what he needed without removing anything from archive storage.

It was all in his mind, but he couldn't get out of his head. The only thing that would manage to get him caught would be his nervous appearance. If he acted guilty, someone would wonder what he had done. That could lead to an investigation, and he hated to think of where that might lead him. It was against the Authority's protocol to access records without permission. He'd done far more than that; he had stolen them.

The papers stayed in his briefcase until he made it home that evening. They haunted him the rest of his shift. Every footstep he heard in the hall made his breath stop as he waited for a Security member to barge in to take him in for questioning. The ringing of the phone on his desk would startle him and send him off his seat in the air. Each noise was a sign of his impending undoing. It was only a matter of time until the Authority discovered what he had done, until Security came for him. One of these noises would be it, but he had no way to tell how soon it would come.

When Phillipe finally made it to the privacy of his own home, he took his briefcase to the table and laid the papers out before him. He could see them. He could recognize the combination of letters on them as words, but he couldn't make out anything more than that. The excitement was too immense for him to concentrate.

All of these years, he had barely any information about his parents. There was only what the Authority saw fit to tell him, and that was very little. It all amounted to a handful of facts. Dates of their births and deaths, their names, how they died, and a painting in a hall of his father was all he had of his parents. These pages contained so much more. There would be his father's records, detailed reports on any major events, and it was hard to say what information had been gathered on his mother. She had been human. The only reason she had a file at all is because she gave birth to a half breed monster of the Below.

The excitement was there, but also fear. It wasn't merely the fear of getting caught. Phillipe was afraid of the unknown. The information contained in these papers could make him long for the childhood he never had even more than he already did. There could be details that might shape an image of his parents in a way he had never imagined. It always seemed odd to miss two people and have so much love for them when you never knew them. This was his chance. By the end of the night, he would know more about them than he had learned over the centuries.

What he did not expect was to learn everything he'd ever been told was a lie. The Authority had covered up the truth about his parents. The reasons why they kept it hidden weren't included in the paperwork, but the why wasn't important. It wouldn't change the fact that no one felt the Jacobys' own son should know what really happened.

It felt like an insult to his parents' memory. It was a slight against his father's name, and he made the decision that night to rectify it. He wasn't sure how he would manage to get to the surface, but he would avenge them if it was the last thing he did.

Chapter Thirteen

Wolfsbane

Masterson sat behind his desk staring across his office at nothing in particular. The reports coming in couldn't be correct, but he knew they had to be. Jacoby had escaped. Jacoby. Had. Escaped.

The runt had lived longer than almost anyone currently in the Below. Aside from a few minor disciplinary problems growing up that amounted to not much more than being a young punk, there had never been anything about him to stand out as a potential threat. He'd gone through his required review every decade without a fuss. Unlike a lot of lifers down here, he went before the board every time. That was something Masterson always admired about him. The little guy never gave up even if the outcome was certain.

This last review he had taken it a step farther and filed an appeal. It should've set off a red flag then. The Security office, his office, should've recognized it as a potential threat and investigated what was so important to him that made the need to go to the surface that immense after centuries of compliance. Masterson had missed it. He saw it as nothing more than Jacoby enjoying the few freedoms living in the Below provided. It was the right of every citizen to appeal the board's decision. It would've helped too if Lichten had reported the outburst from Jacoby when his appeal had been denied.

It would do no good to dwell on the should've, would've, could've now. The time to analyze where they failed would come to pass. Every action would be scrutinized, and every missed step would be found and handled. New protocols may be enacted if necessary. Now was not the time for it. All that mattered right now was Jacoby.

Jacoby had waited too long. If he had been appealing the decisions since the beginning, he probably would've made the vertical move in the Middle Ages. The state of the world Above had changed too much. It was becoming more and more dangerous for any of these cryptoids to live amongst the rest of the world. The criteria to be approved was becoming stricter, and the Above Guard weren't taking chances either. Minor offenses were sending creatures back down for good.

The population of the Below was past its capacity because of it. Hard decisions were going to have to be made soon. The punishment for making a mistake upstairs might not be a ticket back for much longer. It may have to be a more permanent end to any more potential wrong doing.

Humans weren't stupid. Well, not all of them were at any rate. Their eyes were opening to the hidden world around them. They were seeing the fairies that spirited about in the gardens. The traces of evidence some beasts left behind were no longer simply explained away. The humans wanted answers. They wanted the truth. All it would take would be one capture. If one of these creatures that the Security and the Guard had sworn to protect were ever captured, the surface relocation housing program would be over. There wasn't enough room to bring everyone back.

People wouldn't stop with one, and everyone in power agreed on that. They would continue to dig, figuratively speaking, until the entire Below community was exposed. Closed door meetings had been in process since midway through the twentieth century to set emergency lock down protocols into place. It didn't matter what name they labeled these sessions. The purpose of the meetings was to determine how to dispose of those already settled upstairs when the time came.

That's why Jacoby was denied the appeal. Masterson admired the poor sap. If he had appealed a century ago, maybe less, he'd be up top. His timing was off. That bad timing was what had just signed his death certificate. Whatever he was after upstairs had to be more valuable than life itself, and learning what it was would be the key to his capture.

For now, Masterson had to face the escape. That word jumped down Masterson's gullet every time it was spoken and violently attacked him from the inside out. The Below was supposed to be an inescapable fortress. It always had been. Many had tried, but none had ever succeeded until now. Jacoby was the first, and he would be the last. There was no question of that. The only reservation anyone had was whether he'd be brought in by the Guard where hopefully no damage to the thin cover of their existence would be committed, or if he'd be found out by the people of Rotterdam bringing a world of hurt raining down on all of the cryptoids alive, upstairs or down.

A knock on the open office door broke Masterson free of his thoughts. "Yes?" he bellowed.

Officer Gordy sheepishly stuck his head in the door. "You wanted me to report back to you when I returned," he said with uncertainty.

Masterson sank back in his chair and nodded. "Strickland is dead?" he asked for clarification.

"Yes," Gordy answered, holding his hat in his hands and shifting his weight.

"Suicide," Masterson shook his head. Strickland had always been a stand-up guy and came from a proud lycan lineage. It made no sense, but the entire day hadn't made any sense for that matter. "How?"

"He hung himself," Gordy said, looking nervously at his feet.

Masterson rubbed his forehead. He was trying hard to keep his temper contained, but his blood boiled beneath the surface. It bewildered him how the entire department collectively lost their minds when faced with the biggest challenge of their careers. "Werewolves cannot die from hanging, Gordy. It was a trick, and he's escaped you."

"No, sir," Gordy insisted. "His body is in the morgue."

"What are you not telling me?" Masterson said through gritted teeth.

Gordy's eyes darted around the room. If he could have disappeared into the walls, he would have.

"What?" Masterson's voice raised almost to a shout.

"Wolfsbane," Gordy said.

Several stunned moments passed. Wolfsbane was banned from the Below. As with all contraband, it had found its way into the hands of citizens from time to time. The razing of the garden of the witch Astrid in 1879 was believed to have eradicated it for good. "How can you be sure?"

Gordy reached into his hat and removed a small vial. He slowly walked to Masterson's desk and set it down. Several small purple flowers remained inside.

Masterson stared at it as though they were dangerous to the touch. "Tell me everything," he ordered, not lifting his eyes from the vial.

He continued to stare at the flowers inside of the glass almost as if they were the first actual cryptoid he'd ever encountered. They were certainly rarer and supposedly non-existent in their world. He only half heard the tale Gordy was repeating, but he caught enough to follow.

Strickland was remorse when they arrived. He'd been expecting the Security team to come for him. They didn't notice the noose because they hadn't searched the premises. He was waiting for them in the front room. Jacoby promised Wolfsbane in exchange for access to the water pipes, but he put it into Strickland's tea as well. Once he drank it, the transformation began. He couldn't over power Jacoby when he attacked him and stole the key card. He was too weak from his rebirth. The Wolfsbane was never meant for him. It was for his grandmother who was growing too weak for the lunar cycle transitions.

"He told us everything and said he'd come willingly. When he stood, he darted into the darkness. We searched the rooms prepared for him to fight his capture. The electricity had been disabled which hindered our search. By the time we found him, he was dead."

Masterson picked up the vial and turned it over in his hands. The puzzle was growing ever more complicated. Where did Jacoby manage to get his hands on Wolfsbane?

Chapter Fourteen

It's All Routine

The pounding on the door of his loft mimicked the deafening staccato his heart had been beating in his chest since Phillipe appeared in his store that morning. All of the creatures of the Below would be subject to a search. It only stands to reason that one of them would be willingly to help one of their own. They both knew it was only a matter of time before the Guard made an appearance, but John had expected it sooner than later.

Escapes from the Below simply did not occur. The few who attempted it over the years were never seen again. Security would issue a statement of their arrest and incarceration, but there was talk. There was always gossip about the actual fate they met. While Security would want for all to believe escape attempts resulted in life in prison, the citizens of the Below believed the punishment was death.

Never had an escape attempt been successful. The laws of the Below were taught in school every year for all seven grades they were required to attend. Anyone who chose, or could afford, to attend secondary school toiled through two semesters of Below history and government in a more disciplined environment.

Still, some details were forgotten by all over time. The phrase use it, or lose it wasn't isolated to the Above alone. Most of the laws were precautionary and had never been broken at least not in any living creature's memory. That was true of escapes. In later discussions throughout his life, John would learn every creature he talked to about it, and it was a hot topic of conversation for decades, had surmised the punishment would be death.

Another thing everyone had in common regarding Jacoby's escape is no one had been able to recall the protocol for such a crime. It had been taught to them in depth year after year, but they were unable to pull even one piece of that information to the front of their minds. Most of them, John included, scrambled to find the paperwork and guides they had been issued when they transferred to the surface to refresh themselves on what to expect.

For the rest of them, it was a morbid curiosity. It was a fascination that someone actually managed the impossible. They may have had a slight question of how it could affect them, but mainly they wondered what punishment the escapist would face.

John had the most to lose. Jacoby had attached himself to John's side, and made countless threats about what would happen if John didn't help him. He didn't threaten to harm John of course. It was his girlfriend Christine who would suffer if John didn't comply.

The Guard would do a preliminary search of all creature's homes and businesses within a certain radius of where Jacoby escaped. As they dug into their search and learned more about him, building a profile, they would revisit those they felt might be apt to aide a criminal, this criminal.

Phillipe told him it would be routine. There would be a few simple questions to answer and possibly a quick search of his apartment then they'd be on their way to the next address. That's what he assured John as he left to go to the home of Christine's parents where she lived.

How quickly he forgot the reason John was granted permission to ascend. The Guard wouldn't be coming for a quick search. They were coming to involve John's help in apprehending Jacoby. He was sure of it.

The pounding came again only harder this time which he wouldn't thought was possible. It jolted him from his thoughts. Along with the fists banging on the door, he could hear someone shouting. "Reed! We know you're in there!"

"Coming," he said. His voice barely managed to rise above a whisper. He cleared his throat while standing up and tried again. "Coming!"

The walk to the door was slow and treacherous. The near over exhaustion of his heart made it difficult to time his steps without tripping, and a sudden dizziness came over him adding to the difficulty he had walking.

'Get it together,' he chided himself. *'They're going to take one look at you and know of your involvement.'*

He slid the upper lock back and turned the dead bolt then started to open the door slowly. One of the two Guard members on the other side gripped the edge of the door and forced it wide almost knocking John over in the process.

They were both male, wearing street clothes. That had been another curiosity. What secret identities would the Guard team who showed up portray? They were all plants in the human world. They could appear as detectives, housewives, salesmen, anybody really. That's how they managed to keep such a keen eye on those they swore to protect.

Swore to spy on was more like it, but it was part of the tradeoff for fresh air and sunshine. There was a line between keeping their kind safe and being in control of their lives. It was a line that always seemed blurred, and for those who rose above the surface, it never tilted in their favor.

"Where is he?" the man who forced the door open asked. His black graphic tee shirt half untucked, making him appear so much less than his position warranted.

"Who?" John asked.

"Don't play games, Reed," the second man said, following the first into the apartment.

John shook his head. "Sorry. Force of habit. I haven't seen him."

The first man took a deep breath and loudly exhaled, letting the air blow through his lips. "Simmons," he said, giving a one name introduction. "This is Boyd," he said, nodding to his partner.

"He hasn't been in contact?" Boyd asked.

"No," John lied. His conscious was screaming at him to tell the truth, but he couldn't risk anything happening to Christine. More so, he couldn't risk her finding out the truth about him. Not in this way. Plus he had no idea what the Guard would do to her if she found out about him and freaked out. Dating a human was a serious concern to the Guard. If a person was to be introduced to their world, the Guard handled it. No exceptions.

"You don't mind if I look around then?"

John shook his head then uttered, "No."

While Boyd searched his apartment, Simmons got straight to it. "The search is standard. The residences of all Below citizens will be cleared until Jacoby's capture, but that's not the real reason we're here."

"I expected this," John nodded.

Simmons arched an eyebrow. "So you know what we're going to ask?"

This was it. This was what he felt like he had been bred for his entire life. His passion was baking, but his genetics made him perfect for a number of other roles. "You want me to help you capture him."

"Slow down there, partner," Boyd said, returning from the bedroom. He cracked a smile at Simmons and added, "We're far from recruiting a hero at this point."

Simmons looked irritated but agreed. "Currently, we're confident he'll turn up within the hour. We believe he's being assisted by a friend he made downstairs. We'll flush them out."

John nodded. There really wasn't much else he could say when the truth was off the table.

"In the rare event that we don't," Simmons continued, "we need to make sure you're still on board to be of service if we need you."

"Yes, of course," John said.

Simmons stared off across the living room. He tapped

the tip of the thumb on his left hand to his fingertips beginning with his index finger down to his pinky and back again repeatedly.

The apartment was silent. Even the breeze that had been gently blowing the curtains of the open window halted, recognizing the gravity of the situation. John held his breath subconsciously until he loudly sucked a gasp of air into his lungs a minute later. He didn't know what was going through Simmons' mind, or his partner's. Once they were gone, he'd be able to breathe easy was the lie he told himself. Even then, he knew it wouldn't be over. He wouldn't be safe. Christine wouldn't be safe until Jacoby was caught, and he was more worried about what Jacoby would do to them for betraying him than what the Guard would hand down as punishment for abetting.

"Why aren't you on the team?" Simmons asked.

"What?"

Simmons circled around to face him. "This ability of yours... It makes you well suited for our line of work. Why is it that you never applied to either the Above or the Below's forces?"

'Oh, this,' John thought. *'It was a question he'd been skirting most of his life.'*

"It was never the dream," he answered truthfully. "It wasn't for me."

"Before we go further, we need to be sure," Boyd said. "We can't make any guarantees."

Simmons looked annoyed with his partner again. "What he's trying to say is we'll do the best we can, but we can't guarantee your safety."

John nodded.

"Are you sure you understand?"

"Yes," John answered quietly.

Taking one last look around the room, Simmons put his hands on his hips and asked, "Why? Why risk everything?"

"It was a condition of my move," John admitted.

The two detectives exchanged glances. John sucked in his breath. They had obviously not been made aware of that detail, and he worried he let something slip he shouldn't have.

"I see," Simmons said, making his way toward the door. "We'll be in touch."

John saw them out, but before he closed the door on them, Boyd turned around and said the first thing that didn't seem out of hand since he arrived. "I'm sure Jacoby will be in custody by nightfall. This," he said, waving his hands between himself and John, "it was all routine. Nothing to get yourself riled up about."

Chapter Fifteen

Just a Dream

When she woke up that morning, Christine inhaled the sunshine and the scent of wildflowers drifting into her room off the breeze. Her smile had been painted on her face for days ever since John asked her out to Sixteen Waterside. It was the restaurant too expensive to afford a name, so it used its address instead. That was the joke anyway. There were only two kinds of people who dined there. The filthy rich could afford it any time they chose, but John was certainly not in that category. Everyone else went there to celebrate milestone anniversaries or to get engaged. It was happening tonight. She could feel it.

Watching a belligerent man rummage through her parents' kitchen was the last thing she expected to do today. Yet, here she was doing exactly that. He had tried to drink ketchup and Italian dressing straight from the bottle before finding the half bottle of strawberry flavored water Christine had put in the refrigerator last night. It's like this guy crawled out from under a rock somewhere. John would have a lot of explaining and making up to her later.

He had at least sent a warning text. It didn't make too much sense when she first read it. "An old friend is stopping by - Phillipe - Just please go along with him - I'm so sorry - I love you so much."

Christine wasn't sure what he was trying to say. She thought he might have been canceling their dinner plans. It could've just as easily read like John wanted her to entertain some friend of his for the evening. It'd be a cold day in hell.

He didn't answer when she called to find out what he was talking about. The seven texts she sent after the missed call went unanswered as well. She was on her way out the door to his apartment when this clown showed up. He was on the doorstep, arm raised, preparing to knock when she opened the door and jumped, shocked to see anyone there.

"Christine," he cooed.

The way he said her name like they were old friends churned her stomach when she had never seen this guy in her life. "Who the hell are you?" she asked. Her anger with her boyfriend spilling out at the stranger.

This is the part that should read there was a struggle, but that's not true. The guy raised his fist, and Christine cowered. "Take whatever you want!" she offered. She pulled her wallet from her purse and threw it at him.

His feet went passed her while she crouched on the floor crying and trying to figure out how to unlock her phone. The tears streaming from her eyes prevented the facial recognition from working. She made several attempts to enter her passcode, but messed it up each time.

There was some way to make an emergency call while the phone was still locked. Christine couldn't remember the number of times the prompt to make that call appeared on her screen accidentally. *'Oh, no. No!'* she would think. She would quickly move to get that option off her phone. *'Let's not call the police.'* Now the moment had arrived when she actually did need to make an emergency call while her phone was locked, and she couldn't for the life of her figure out how to do it.

The guy who had barged into her home reappeared and snatched the phone from her hands. "Almost forgot about this," he said. "Not used to these yet."

He grabbed her arm and lifted her off the floor. "Come," he ordered.

Christine followed him down the hall never questioning why she didn't run out the front door until later. The assumption that he would hurt her was there based on his threat of hitting her. There was the odd text from John calling this guy an old friend. It created a twisted curiosity when he said he wasn't familiar with cell phones. Everyone knows their way around one. Mostly, it was that it never occurred to her in her frightened state that she had the option to run.

She followed him into the kitchen where he repeatedly turned the knobs on the sink. He pulled on the spout hard enough she thought it might break. "How do you work this?" he asked with growing irritation.

"The water is off," she told him.

The strange man straightened and stared ahead. He inhaled and exhaled slowly in an attempt to quell his anger. "I can see that it is off," he told her through clenched teeth. "How do you turn it on?"

"No," she explained. "A pipe burst in the basement last night. The water is off to the house until the plumber comes this afternoon."

He punched the nearest cabinet hard enough to crack the entire face of it then turned to her.

"I don't know how to turn it back on," she said, stepping backward.

The man strung together a slur of obscenities and punched the counter repeatedly before moving to the refrigerator. That's when he had trouble finding something to drink.

This had to be a prank. Someone was putting her on. There were too many oddities about this guy, but he didn't otherwise act like it was caused by drugs, mental illness, or anything else she might recognize. He spoke coherently and even introduced himself after finally finding something to quench his thirst. Then he moved on to the microwave, opening and shutting the door like he had never seen one and was trying to figure out its purpose. While he stood there playing with it, Christine watched as he appeared to grow taller.

It was a dream. Of course, she was dreaming. There could be no other explanation. She pulled out a stool and sat at the counter waiting to see what twists and turns her subconscious would take with it next.

"So, Phillip," she began.

"Phillipe," he corrected.

"Phil-lip," she enunciated. She knew she was saying it wrong and would probably upset him, but a dream couldn't hurt her.

"Phil-leap!" he yelled.

She shrugged. "Whatever. How do you know John?"

"I think the real question is, how well do *you* know him?"

This wasn't a rabbit hole she was willing to go down, not even when she was asleep. It wouldn't do her relationship any good for seeds of doubt to be planted, awake or not.

Christine stood up to get some breakfast, but Phillipe cut her off before she made it two steps from the stool.

"What do you think you're doing?" he asked.

It startled her, and she wondered why it hadn't been enough to wake her. "I was going to get a yogurt," she said.

"Sit," he ordered. He went across the room and grabbed it for her.

It was definitely a dream. His head came to the top of the freezer now when he had barely stood taller than the refrigerator door while he was looking for something to drink.

Chapter Sixteen

Unauthorized Access

Reports started coming in from all over. Masterson would no sooner get off one phone call then his computer would chime out a notification of a new email, or someone would radio on the walkie talkie. Everything had come up empty so far, everything except Gordy's visit with Strickland.

There was Wolfsbane in the Below which was quite worrisome. It wasn't as simple as it sounded. The cure for lycanthrophy came at a cost. The argument had always been to leave it up to the individual to decide, but Wolfsbane could be weaponized against a number of other creatures in the Below. Finding the source was definitely the number one order of business once Jacoby was located. He couldn't spare the manpower until his capture.

He had hoped for a lead by now whether it be video of Jacoby, a witness coming forward claiming Jacoby had been asking odd questions before he disappeared, or some small clue he might have left behind at his house. Masterson simply wanted a lead, any lead, so he could follow up. Then he got the call he'd been waiting on.

The boss of the R & T department phoned to say they had finished the audit on Jacoby's work computer. He had accessed the files of a Brendan Roth without authorization twice.

'*Brendan Roth,*' Masterson thought. The name sounded familiar, but he couldn't place it. There had been too many citizens come and go for him to stay on top of all of them.

"When did Jacoby access it?"

"There were two incidents," the man said. "Once was a little over a year ago. Jacoby filled out the incident report himself. He stated that when typing in a file identification number, he switched a couple of digits, accessing the Roth file by mistake. As soon as he realized what he had done, he closed out of it."

"Why was this never investigated?" Masterson asked.

"It was," the man said. "At the time, and by me as well when I discovered it earlier today. It checks out. He was authorized to access a file number similar to Roth's. The time stamps show he was only in the file for seconds. Jacoby claimed as soon as he saw the address was in Rotterdam and not in Buenos Aires as he expected, he double checked the file number, realized his mistake, and that was it."

There was a pause as Masterson processed what he was hearing. There had to be more to it. "And the second time? Did it check out as well?"

"Just before he left work on his last shift here. End of the month audits haven't been conducted to flag it yet."

"And it was just as quick?"

"Slightly longer," Jacoby's boss admitted. "And that time,

he printed it entirely."

"Bring me a copy of the file," Masterson ordered.

"I already have an assistant on the way to your office with it, and the information has been sent Above as well."

Masterson hung up the phone and leaned back, resting his elbow on the arm of his chair. *'This can't be as random as you would have us believe,'* he thought. Jacoby's psych evaluations show he wasn't so imbalanced he would open a file accidentally, and make note of it just in case he went off the rails a year later and needed a random target. There's more to it than that.

Case assignments had always been by chance. The question that plagued Masterson now was how long had Jacoby sat on Roth's file number waiting for the right opportunity to come along. He wouldn't be surprised if he wasn't thoroughly impressed with Jacoby's long game by the time this was over.

The file that was delivered was thick without the added bulk of the manila folder and dividers padding it out. Masterson knew as he watched the employee carry it across the room to his desk that Roth had to be an immortal. A file that size could only mean one of two things. Either he had lived long enough to amass multiple lifetime's worth of records, or he was a trouble maker. If the latter were true, the Guard would have dealt with him already.

He dismissed the employee with a smile when she set the pile of papers on his desk with no remorse for not knowing her name. He slid the stack around one hundred and eighty degrees and glanced over the first page for the information he needed.

'Rothstein, Brendr.'
'Roth, Brendis.'
'Roth, Brendan.'

In the upper left of the first page in large, bold type was one word: Vampir. *'That would explain it,'* Masterson thought.

He was disappointed in himself for not recognizing Roth's name what with there being so few vampires left. It tends to happen when the last remaining female of the species dies. Cross breeding with humans had proven to be very tricky.

Any time a species managed to do it successfully was very rare and gained them instant notoriety in the Below. It requires the human to have a specific gene. The marker is so scarce the genome project these people had been working on for decades hadn't identified it yet. It was a lingering remnant of a very distant past where somewhere in their lineage they had descended from a cryptid, and not just any cryptid either.

The ancestors of any humans with this genetic link dated back millenniums ago, long before the Below was built. It's how the Authority has no tracking set up for them. There have yet to be any spontaneous mutant births. The only viable pregnancies between one of their creatures and a human is when the human bears this ancient genetic link to their world.

Masterson scanned each page carefully looking for a link to Jacoby. He had hoped the two men knew each other from the Below. Vampires had been sent to the surface during Jacoby's lifetime. It wouldn't be enough to explain the sudden renewed interest in an old friend or foe, but it was enough to establish a possible connection. Roth was far too old for them to have grown up together, and his ascension was before Jacoby's lifetime. The two would've never met, would've never known of each other's existence.

'But Jacoby did,' Masterson reminded himself. He refused to believe this was coincidence. Jacoby was not on a kamikaze mission, planning on taking out a random creature he stumbled upon accidentally as he went.

It was taking longer than he'd like. The constant interruptions from Security reporting back with nothing to account didn't help. He had to be careful not to move too fast. If he finished without the smallest grain of motive found within this file, he'd have to start over again. If he missed something the first time through it, no matter how seemingly unimportant, it could be enough of a delay to cost Roth his life.

Masterson was easily a third of the way through the sizable file when a bold heading caught his attention: Above Incident Report. Very few occurrences upstairs managed to end without a one way ticket south. Their cover was too precious and too vulnerable to take any risks on second chances.

The date was listed near the start of the report, and Masterson began turning the page. It happened far too long ago to be of relevance. Math wasn't his strong suit, but he didn't think Jacoby had been born at that time. It was also a good indicator of why Roth had been allowed to stay put.

There was a time when the world was less populated. The tales people concocted with drink in hand surrounded by friends were far more entertaining than any accurate description of a run in with a real cryptoid. Plus, they ran from the scent of other worldly danger. They ran from their own fear of things that go bump in the night. If a creature stepped out of line mildly, they might find themselves relocated, and that was usually more than enough to solve the problem.

Today's transplants wouldn't be so lucky. People had grown to be brazen, and bold, and stupid. They would chase after the fairies playing in the garden without the slightest indication of what they would endure if they caught one. Every individual had a phone in their hands at the ready to take pictures or video. The internet connected the globe in deciphering clues of the unknown and examining all proof people claimed to have. One step out of line nowadays could just as easily land a creature in a medical lab never to return as anything else. It's happened more than Masterson cared to remember.

As he was flipping the page over, there was a word that jumped out at him. *'No,'* he thought. *'I read that wrong.'*

He turned it back and began skimming through the type. *'Cargo ship,'* he sighed. It wasn't off to a good start.

Stow away. The words jumped off the page at him. He had heard the gossip when he was coming up in school like most had. There was only one hydrohomunculus left, and that wasn't the only reason he was a morbid fascination among the children. Everyone had heard about how the water dragon Kayda saved the poor babe from certain death, giving up her own freedom to do so.

Then his eyes saw what he was looking for, what he had

hoped he wouldn't find. "It resulted in the death of Jacoby, Roark," Masterson read out loud.

There'd be no stopping him. If Jacoby was on a revenge mission for his parents, Roth had better pray the Guard get to him first.

Chapter Seventeen

Fraternizing with the Enemy

John closed the door and leaned his back against it. He waited and listened as the footsteps retreated down the stairs. His mind told him, *'That was close,'* but he knew there was nothing close about it. It had been easy aside from his ever growing anxiety that he was going to ruin his life, and possibly the lives of his friends, because of one crazed creature from the deep.

He sent Christine a text telling her he was sorry for the fourth time that morning with just as many unanswered calls. There hadn't been a response from her. For the first time in their relationship, he hoped she was ignoring him because she was angry with him. With Phillipe at her house, the alternative would be so much worse. Then he sent another text directing her to tell Phillipe it was over and to call him.

If he had been smart, he would've refused him at the bakery. It wasn't packed when Phillipe showed up, but there would have been witnesses, several of them. He had a chance then. There was a slim opportunity to overpower Phillipe if one of his customers turned out to be a Good Samaritan. When the emergency notification from the Guard was sent to his phone, he would've only had to push one button. That's it. One touch of the screen, and the Guard would've been on its way.

There was a chance Phillipe could have become enraged and done some damage to the bakery, to him. That's not what prevented him from doing anything. He hadn't been afraid.

The only reason he was in the Above was because of the advice given to him by the man randomly appointed to his case for the review. He felt he owed him everything, and he stupidly thought Phillipe wouldn't put his future, his life at risk.

There was still no response from Christine. Something was wrong. He headed out and tried her again, but it went to voice mail after four rings. It was six blocks to her house, but it was about four blocks if he cut through the pharmacy parking lot and the Hansen's yard. He could make it to her house in ten minutes easily. It would take less than five if he ran. He took off clumsily, trying Christine's phone the entire way.

John knocked on Christine's front door loudly, and the door swung open beneath his hand. This wasn't a good sign. "Christine!" he yelled. It was hard to make his voice carry. He was still winded from his sprint. Now was a hell of a time to realize how out of shape he actually was.

He waited a beat, but with no immediate response, he ran into her house, straight toward the stairs thinking he'd check her room first. His feet skipped the first two steps, but when his right foot came down on the third, he heard her voice calmly say, "John," somewhere from the first floor.

It startled him, and he lost his focus. His foot came down wrong as he tried to halt his momentum mid-stride. It slipped off the step, and he came down hard, banging his knee on the stair. The rest of his body followed, and he hit his chin on a higher step. He would've slipped down to the floor not far below if his right hand didn't keep a firm grip on the rail like it was life or death. A steady stream of curse words flowed through his teeth at each new sharp twinge of pain from another body part forcefully hitting wood. When he finally collected himself, he stood up to see Christine and Phillipe staring at him like they were watching an adult man splashing about the shallow end of the swimming pool in fear of drowning.

"You're okay?" he asked.

Her eyes widened, and she countered, "Are *you* okay?"

John took a step toward her, but stopped suddenly lifting his leg and placing his hand on his knee. He took a quick intake of breath when the sharp pain belted out a reminder of his recent fall. From the corner of his eye, he saw the smirk forming on Phillipe's face.

"I've been trying to get ahold of you. I thought something was wrong."

"What would be wrong?" Christine asked with squinted eyes. She took a bite out of the sandwich she was holding before glancing back at Phillipe.

He shrugged at her and shook his head. Then the two of them disappeared through the doorway where they had been standing and headed back to the kitchen.

John didn't know what to think. He was happy Christine appeared to be fine. He was thankful she wasn't harmed. To see them like this, like they were getting along, it irritated him. It made him sick to his stomach. He didn't know what happened after Phillipe arrived here, but he needed to find out.

He limped his way into the kitchen to join them. He stopped a couple times to stretch and bend his knee, hoping to work out whatever he had done to it easily. They were across the counter from each other, having a meal, and laughing like they had picked up their conversation right where they left off with no care at all about John's abrasive entrance.

"So you're telling me," Christine laughed. "Fairies are real, but they are annoying, awful little creatures?" Her eyes watered on the verge of tears.

Phillipe's mouth was full, but he nodded his head violently. He swallowed and washed it down with a swig from a bottle. John wasn't sure what he was drinking, but it didn't look like he could grow any taller.

"Yeah," Phillipe nodded. He ran his tongue along his teeth removing bits of food that were stuck on them. "If you had even one fairy in your yard, you'd spend your mornings cursing the neighbor's dog or the kids that lived down the street."

Christine continued to laugh. "But peppermint? That's how to get rid of them?"

"Any kind of mint," Phillipe said. "Plant it, sprinkle it, you could even throw a handful of breath mints on the lawn. They'd be gone."

She finally took notice of John who had come up beside her. "Oh, honey," she cooed, leaning her head to gently touch his arm for a moment. "We have a lot to discuss."

He couldn't be sure what hurt worse. His knee ached. There was a throbbing in his left wrist which was new. He hadn't noticed it until he rubbed his temples for the thumping migraine that had pounced immediately once he realized Phillipe was filling his girlfriend in on their secrets.

"Why did you never tell her, John?"

Phillipe's voice only caused his head to pound louder. He opened his eyes and glared at him. "You know why," he spat.

Minutes passed, and no one said another word. Christine's laughter slowed and eventually stopped. Tension fell over them, and he feared they thought he had killed the mood. *'Rightfully so!'* he screamed internally at Phillipe.

"Look, I'm just saying I figured you would've trusted her enough-" Phillipe began.

"No," John interrupted him.

"So you don't trust her?" Phillipe asked.

Christine's gaze seared into his skin. "Don't put words in my mouth. You know the rules. You know what could happen now!"

"Don't be so dramatic, John. It's not becoming." Phillipe blew him off and walked back to the refrigerator, grabbing the fixings for a second sandwich. "Have you tried this?" he asked, holding up a package of deli roast beef. "They are really missing out downstairs."

John looked at Christine, pleading with his eyes although even he didn't know what he was begging. The room started to spin. This couldn't be happening.

Everything he had been working for, his bakery, his future with her, it was all at risk.

She patted the stool next to her, and he sat down. "Your friend didn't know you hadn't told me. Don't be mad at him," she said.

His eyes shut tight at the words *your friend*. Phillipe was anything but his friend. "How much do you know?"

"Everything," she said.

He looked at her questioningly. There was no way Phillipe had told her everything. That would take a lot more time.

"Well, the basics at least," Phillipe said. "She knows about you and me, where we're from, and she knows that I'm not supposed to be here."

John put his face in his hands. It was all gone. Rather, it would all be gone soon. His entire life destroyed in less than a day.

"We got off on the wrong foot," Christine admitted. "But once he explained he had been worried I'd turn him in," she laughed. "Of course, then he had to fill me in on what I would be turning him in over."

Phillipe smacked his lips together, chewing loudly, and nodded. "Yeah, it all came out."

"When I couldn't get ahold of you, I thought..." John shook his head. He didn't know what to think anymore.

"Oh, yeah," Phillipe said, pulling Christine's phone from the pocket of the sweats John recognized as his. "About that." He set it down on the counter in front of her. The screen lit up showing the two dozen or so notifications from her boyfriend.

"I thought he was your friend?" Christine asked. "Why were you so worried?"

"Yeah, John." Phillipe gulped from his bottle again. "Why were you?" His eyes sparkled, showing his delight in John's awkward position.

Chapter Eighteen

That Was Then

Children can be cruel. Those words had been spoken to him so often. He could recognize the look on the teacher's or aide's face when they were ready to say it. Yes, children can be cruel, but it doesn't mean they should. The other kids were never punished. They never lost free time or dessert. They were never even subjected to a stern lecture. Those kids could be as mean as they wanted toward him, and they got away with it. If he stood up for himself, he was the one in the wrong. It was Phillipe who suffered the punishment.

It didn't take him long to learn he hated it here. There had to be better in the Above waiting for him. He couldn't wait until the day came when he could leave. He was immortal, but also human like. It meant his turn would take longer than some of the others. It took longer for immortals to understand certain lessons. The value of time and the fragility of life didn't hit in the same way for them. They'd be well into a chosen career before the Authority deemed them of age for consideration to ascend. Many of them had grandchildren before it was a possibility which usually affected their mindset of whether or not they wanted to leave.

Not all children attended school. They were the lucky ones. Phillipe loved school actually. It gave him a break from the agony he went through the rest of the time in the beginning. The ones who weren't forced to attend were the ones whose lifespan didn't warrant it. That's why he thought they were lucky. Their suffering was brief.

The children who attended school didn't start as early as they did upstairs. It was expected that their fundamentals would be taught at home. Children were supposed to show up on the first day of year one with the ability to read, write, and understand basic math. Most of them had loving parents who read to them at night and taught them fractions while baking cookies.

It wasn't the childhood Phillipe experienced. The orphanage was centered on the focal concept of meeting the basic needs of youth until they could be placed into homes. Many of the faces who came through the door didn't have a chance to sleep in their bed before interest had peaked in their adoption.

The Below took care of their own. When some unfortunate event robbed a child of their parents, others of their kind would scramble to take them in and raise them. No one gave thought to what would happen to a child who was the last of their species until Phillipe came along. They hadn't had reason to.

In his opinion, they continued to not give much thought to it after his arrival because the orphanage was where he stayed until reaching adulthood. There were long stretches where he was the only child there. By his teens, they'd leave him for the night. The main rooms were locked up, preventing him from snooping or sneaking into the kitchen for snacks. It never crossed his mind to do either. He enjoyed the solitude. It was, after all, a preview of how his life would play out. There would be many people in his life, but at the end of the day, he would always be alone.

He had been looking forward to school. He wanted to make friends and learn as much as he could about everything. The staff had worn themselves tired telling him story after story about anything that came to mind. He hung on every word, never learning enough.

The night before his first day, one of the caretakers stayed with him and taught him how to write his name. It had been an oversight on the part of the orphanage. It was the first time a child had been with them for that many years. They never had to prepare a child for school before, and as such, it wasn't a function of their program. Mistress Dawly assured him they'd work together every day to catch him up to the other students. It was only the first day. They wouldn't do much more than introductions and distribution of materials. He shouldn't worry.

He arrived at the small schoolhouse filled with hope and excitement. The chances of ever finding adoptive parents were nil, but his loneliness might finally be erased through new friendships. It wasn't standard for residents of the orphanage to be given permission to leave for playdates and parties, but he was their first permanent resident. He had been assured special allowances would be given to him which as he grew older, he was certain came from their own staffing issues.

All of his expectations were soon destroyed. The students found their assigned seats and introduced themselves one by one as the teacher circled the room, letting each one speak. Then the teacher announced they would do a basic skills test. It wasn't for a grade; it was simply to let her know where everyone was in terms of what they knew and still needed to learn.

A feeling of dread crept up deep inside of him. He tried to push it away. All he could do was write his name in the corner of the page the teacher had instructed each student to pull out from their supplies and place on their desk. He knew he was behind, but he tried his best to quell his anxiety. After class, he would stop at her desk. He would explain to his teacher that Mistress Dawly had promised to help him.

The opportunity would never come. He paid attention to the lessons as best he could, not understanding most of what was being taught. The class marched single file down to the lunchroom, and Phillipe was blown away by the choices made available to them. He had never been given options before and soon discovered he still wasn't offered a choice. As a poor student, his lunch was the basic meal provided for the day. It didn't go unnoticed by him, or by anyone present, that he was the only poor student in that lunch period.

It was fine. He didn't mind. The other children soon brushed it off like it didn't matter either. They weren't given long to finish eating before they were ushered outside to the playground. It was well lit by street lamps all around the border of it. He fit right in with the others. They laughed and teased each other as they scrambled up the ladders to the slides or took turns on the swings. When the playground monitor blew the whistle signaling the end of free time, he walked into the building in the middle of a group of boys, feeling the happiest he'd ever been.

It was short lived. When he entered the classroom, the teacher called him to her desk. She handed him a slip of paper that was folded carefully and asked him to take it to the office.

"Yes, ma'am," he said. "Let me just set my bottle down on my desk," he added.

"That won't be necessary," she said sternly. "Take it with you."

As he left the room, his eyes scanned over his desk. It had been emptied. Something had happened, but he wasn't sure what.

He walked down the hallway, trying hard to remember the way. The office was near the front entrance, but he was having a difficult time remembering which hallway took him there. His heart raced, thinking of every detail of the day. He hadn't got in any trouble, nor had he broke a single rule that wasn't caught right away. Of that, he was sure.

There were other schools in the Below. Perhaps he was being transferred, but it didn't seem like that was the answer. The orphanage was only two blocks away. This was the closest school to him unless... *'No,'* he told himself. *'You haven't been adopted.'*

Less than a minute later, he was walking up to the long counter in the school office. He had to stand on his tip toes to see the secretary over the top. He had tried in vain to erase all thoughts of finding parents from his mind, but he hoped whatever was going on didn't turn out to be too bad.

The secretary smiled at him and took the note he offered. She read it quickly and smiled. "So you're Phillipe Jacoby?" she asked.

He nodded.

"Come with me." She opened the door near the far wall to step out from behind the counter.

Phillipe was confused, and it showed on his face.

"You've been transferred to a different class," she explained when she realized he was still standing in place and not following her out into the hall. "You're belongings have already been moved."

It was a bit of a gut punch. He had made progress toward making friends, and he'd have to start over with a new group of children. He hoped the new class was one of the others that had been on the playground at the same time as his class had been.

He followed the secretary through the building while he gave it more thought. All the first and second years were together for lunch and free period. It would be impossible for him not to be reunited with the kids he met this morning when they went out to play tomorrow. He was smiling and not suspecting anything when his world crashed around him moments later.

Chapter Nineteen

New Class

The new classroom was in the old wing of the building. It was the original school actually. As the Below grew, a new school was built, but the old one remained attached like an arm extending from it. It was only one story, and Phillipe had been told it was run down and not good for anything much more than storage.

As he followed the secretary down the hallway, they passed one darkened room after another. He wasn't tall enough to see through the windows of the rooms with closed doors, but a few of them were open. Still not sure what they were doing in this part of the school, he walked slow enough to take a good look inside when he could without being too slow to cause Ms. Adams, the secretary, to order him to move along. She was a harpy, and he didn't wish to witness her temper up close.

Through these doors, he could see the disarray. Some of the rooms had boxes stacked on the desks. There were broken chairs if there were any chairs at all. Someone had recently been in one of the rooms as there were footprints deep within the dust on the floor.

At the end of the hallway were two rooms across from each other. These doors looked different than the others they had passed. They appeared cleaner, lighter in color somehow. One had light shining from the crack at the bottom, but there was no window. The other had light pouring through the window and at the bottom. It was the only light in the entire hallway except for what managed to illuminate from the newer part of the building they had just left.

Ms. Adams gave that door a quick knock and waited. No one answered or called out, but after a moment, she opened the door all the same. She didn't open it all the way, just enough for her to peek inside. "Mr. Donnelly," she said, "sorry to interrupt."

A loud, booming voice answered her. "It's perfectly fine. Is he with you?"

"Yes."

"Send him in."

She turned to Phillipe, holding the door for him. "Well, off you go then," she said.

"Go where?"

Her eyes squinted quizzically. "To your new classroom, of course. Get a move on." She gently pushed on the back of his shoulder, encouraging him to step inside.

This didn't feel right. All of the first year classrooms were in the same corridor. He wouldn't have guessed he'd be moved this far away.

Hesitantly, he stepped inside and gasped when he saw the room. It was packed. The desks were positioned in an almost unpassable way, using every inch of space in the room. Each one was occupied by a different species of child, and some appeared far too old to be in a class with him. A centaur stood at the front of the room, and he must've been the voice he heard talking to Ms. Adams. As he looked around, he saw his belongings were on the desk the centaur was standing near.

Noticing his gaze, the centaur spoke, "I'm Mr. Donnelly, and this is my classroom. We'll have to figure out the placement of a desk for you, but until then," he patted a stool on the opposite side of the desk from where the teacher would sit, "this will have to do for the short term."

Phillipe didn't move. He stared at the seat Mr. Donnelly wanted him to take then slowly looked around the classroom again. All of the students were staring at him. Some were whispering to each other and pointing in his direction. Others covered their mouths to hide their laughter.

"Quiet!"

Mr. Donnelly's voice was so loud and unexpected it made him jump. The class stopped making any noise and turned their attention to their desks. When Phillipe looked back at his new teacher, he had his arms folded across his chest and was sternly looking in his direction.

He walked over to the teacher's desk and climbed on the stool. There was only one support rung near the bottom of it which made it difficult for Phillipe. He slipped a couple times before managing to get seated. The class snickered behind him again, but one look from Mr. Donnelly silenced them.

Lowering his head closer to Phillipe, the teacher told him, "I see a review of the rules are in order. You'll stay after class to go over them."

It didn't take long for Phillipe to figure out what happened. Just because he didn't know how to read or write more than his name did not mean he was dumb. The teacher was explaining the basics to everyone even the older students. In some of the subjects, there was more than one lesson. He'd start with the easier material then while those students worked, he'd cover something else for the rest of them.

When he handed in the paper with only his name on it that morning, his original teacher had reported it to the office. He realized he should've said something to his teacher on the way to lunch instead of waiting until the end of the day like he planned. The orphanage would be able to straighten it out. Once he told Mistress Dawly what happened, someone would contact the school. That's what he told himself every time he felt like crying. The worst that could happen was he'd be stuck in this class until he caught up, but at least he knew he would be able to catch up to the rest of his grade.

Until then, he'd still see the friends he'd made on the playground since all first years went together. It wasn't the end of the world even if it felt like it. He just had to make it through the rest of today.

Mistress Dawly did contact the school several times. The administrator of the orphanage himself came down and met with the head master. Nothing changed.

The next day he would learn things were far worse than he could've imagined. The lunch bell rang, and he happily jumped up to stand in line. It was the first time he had smiled since returning from the play break the day before. He knew he'd have to stay with his class during lunch, but once they were on the playground, that would change. He couldn't wait to see his new friends.

Mr. Donnelly waited until everyone was ready then opened the door of the classroom, leading all the students out. He led them to the room across the hall. The door had been closed yesterday, so Phillipe had been unable to look inside. It was their cafeteria, their separate, isolated cafeteria. He felt heat flush his face, but he tried not to overreact. Lunches were separated by classroom anyway as far as seating. He knew that. This was disappointing, but it would be fine. At least the lunch break was the same time as the day before. It meant he'd still see his friends soon.

The whole cafeteria experience was different than the one he faced yesterday. Gone were the multiple lines of choices for what to eat, not that he had that luxury. Here, there was only one option. Everyone ate the same thing.

He monitored his breathing, trying to keep his emotions in control. This, too, didn't affect him. He took a deep breath in. As a poor student, he would have to eat the standard lunch every day anyway. Then he slowly exhaled.

The class he had been moved to continued becoming more substandard and second-class. Each time he thought it couldn't get worse, it did. Part of him felt like it had finally reached the bottom of how bad it could get. Part of him worried the hits would keep on coming.

Phillipe rushed through his lunch. He wasn't hungry, and the food that was served could barely pass as having nutritional content. There was plenty of time before the bell would ring for break, but he wanted to be ready. When it was time to head to the playground, he would be the first one in line. And, he was.

When Mr. Donnelly led the children into the hall, he didn't turn to the right, heading the direction Phillipe had followed Ms. Adams yesterday. Instead, he headed left for an exit door at the other end of the hall not far from where they were. For the slightest moment, he panicked. Then he realized it must simply be a shortcut. They would make it to the playground quicker if they walked around the building instead of through it. When the door opened, his world crashed down around him again and exploded into flames.

Chapter Twenty

Stolen Life

He hadn't stayed in the file long. He couldn't. There was so much more information he wanted to know, but it was too risky. If they suspected him of violating Authority rules, he'd be fired. For now, he'd just have to wait. He had been waiting a very long time for this opportunity, displaying a level of patience that surprised him.

Every morning, he checked all of the new case file numbers that had been assigned to him if there were any. Cases were assigned in numerical order by birth and weren't given any special identification by race which was perfect. Eventually, one would come across his desk so close to Roth's it could be plausible Phillipe made a simple mistake when typing it.

It had finally happened. He had been given the case management for a Lilith, another creature who had been given a bad rep. The number was identical to Roth's except hers began with the number 4, and his with a 1. He couldn't believe how easy it would be with the numbers on top of one another on the side keypad. The opportunity had been handed to him on a silver platter after years of waiting.

Roth was living in the city of Rotterdam which wasn't far from some of the tunnels to the surface. The Guard was initializing contact with his fiancé Serena to disclose the details of Roth's supernatural status and his history. If the meeting didn't go well, Roth would be sent back to the Below. Some of the creatures were given another chance and moved elsewhere to start over with new identities, but not vampires. They had been on a one strike and you're out policy for centuries, ever since mayhem shocked its way through Europe over the myths and legends that surrounded the name.

No one ever really spoke of what became of the humans caught in the crossfire. Some were able to handle learning that the creatures of fairy tales and horror stories were real. Others didn't take the news quite so well. They were all given a period to adjust and adapt. It didn't always work out for the best. Files were updated regarding what happened to their own, but news of the human's fate was never disclosed. Everyone had a different theory which all ended in the same result.

It wasn't the ideal circumstances for Phillipe to work with, but he had hope either way. If Serena handled it badly and the Guard was unable to prevent her from drawing unwanted attention to the situation, Roth would be sent back. It would be easier for Phillipe to access him, but he would certainly be caught. He wanted Serena to pass the Guard's scrutiny with flying colors. An escape wouldn't be easy, but he had been planning it since he learned of Roth's involvement with his parents' deaths. It could be done. At least in the Above, he stood the slightest chance of avoiding capture by the Guard.

The thing that irritated him the most about what he learned in the file was Roth's engagement. He had played a role in the death of his parents and was allowed to walk free. The surface didn't take kindly to non-humans, so of course, he was probably hailed a hero by them, but the Guard looked the other way as well. They considered it an unfortunate, but necessary circumstance that Roth participated. It was his choice to do so that night.

It was understandable that he didn't put his own life in danger by intervening to stop it. Phillipe recognized that and didn't fault him for not trying to save his father. With the frantic energy of the sailors and the cover of darkness, he could've shown a fellow cryptoid a small amount of respect by stepping to the side. Instead, he participated in the melee. He said so himself in his account to the Guard concerning the events of that evening. Roth participated in his father's murder, and after Kayda disappeared, he was one of the men who captured his mother.

The Guard determined that no fault would be placed on him as he was acting in his own best interest to keep his true identity safe. He was allowed to go on living like nothing had ever happened. Roth moved around over time to keep his cover a secret. It would be hard to explain his longevity otherwise. In each new home, there was a new marriage. He had finally found a new love who could bare him children. Many more cryptoids born Above, who would always enjoy life Above because of that, to continue his name.

Phillipe had been born Above, yet he's never experienced

a single day of sunshine and fresh air. He had never known the real love of a woman. There'd been stolen kisses with a kelpie, a late night rendezvous with a lamia or a secret affair with a satyr. He'd had his share of physical connections, but nothing that was authentic.

There was a deep, ingrained discrimination in the Below pertaining to inter-species relationships. No one said too much about young lovers having fun, but when it came to the long term, they were expected to marry their own kind. It all boiled down to the continuation of the species. It was the only guaranteed way to have children. Two cryptoid species couldn't reproduce easily. Even having a family with a human was a long shot, but there was a tiny chance.

Phillipe had been robbed of everything. His parents were murdered. He'd never got to know them, had never been held by either of them. Kayda saved his life, yes, but in doing so, she took him to the Below. The death of his father took away his opportunity to grow up on the surface. Never being allowed to return took away his only chance of finding love or having a family.

Meanwhile Roth was handed everything he'd always been denied. There were no repercussions for his actions. He willfully and maliciously assisted in the death of his father, and what he did to his mother was unfathomable. Yet here he was over a thousand years later still living on the surface, probably having long forgotten the horrid existence that was the Below. It had changed so much since Phillipe was a child and not for the better. Roth would have no clue how much worse it had become, the overcrowding, the poorer air quality, and the scarceness of resources.

Phillipe wanted to return the kindness Roth had shown his parents when they were the most vulnerable, bringing a new life into the world. He wanted to see the look on Serena's face when she watched the life leave the eyes of her husband. Then he would take hers, leaving their vampire hybrid babe to grow up in the Below where vampires no longer existed, alone and isolated as he had been. He wanted revenge, and he would have it. Anyone who tried to stand in his way would be removed by any means necessary.

Chapter Twenty-One

Surveillance Footage

The phone rang in Liam's office, and he stared at it for a minute instead of answering. He knew it was Masterson on the other end of the line. It had been Masterson every other time the phone rang today except once, and that was a member of the Guard who had been unable to reach him by radio because Liam had been in the middle of a phone call where he had his backside handed to him by the Director of Below Security. The guard called as soon as Masterson had hung up.

It rang two more times, and he gave in with a sigh. Orders were orders, and like it or not, he did report to the Security Director. Liam had been told in no uncertain terms that he was to stay put, running the command center from his office. It had upset him. This was the first real excitement the Guard had experienced in his lifetime, and he wanted to be in the thick of it. He was going to stick Adam in the office while he went into the field for what was likely to be his only chance to do what he considered real police work, but Masterson had other plans for them, probably due to him rejecting the call that morning. There'd be hell to pay if he missed another one.

He picked it up at the end of the third ring, but it wasn't Masterson's voice on the other end. He exhaled in a huff not realizing he had been holding his breath, but the relief he felt from not being screamed at again didn't last. It ended before the breath of air leaving his lungs did. There was more bad news to report.

Liam listened as Adam updated him about the problems he'd encountered with the surveillance cameras. He heard every word, but his thoughts quickly turned to Phillipe. Either he had been planning this escape every day of his 1347 years of life, or he was the luckiest son of a gun to ever exist.

'No one had ever escaped before, not like this.'

The Guard still wasn't operating at full capacity. Many of his team who had the day off for Patrick's funeral had come in already. They were sleep deprived, having tried to adjust for the change in Below time to attend the funeral. Many more were still waiting to return. Trips to and from the Below were staggered to avoid suspicion. Most humans would notice seeing a group that large disappear into the forest together. As urgent as it was to find Phillipe, the greater good would always be the secrecy of the Below. They had to come back in shifts.

It would be worth investigating more into Patrick's death once Phillipe was found. The timing was too much of a coincidence. It could be just that, a lucky break that the funeral of someone in their field occurred when he was planning to make a run for it. Liam's gut said otherwise.

Word had traveled to him that Phillipe had managed to get his hands on Wolfsbane. It was outlawed in the Below and tracked up here, but somehow he had it to bribe a member of Security. He had a feeling when Patrick's cause of death was looked at with more scrutiny, it would no longer be declared a heart attack.

"The camera at the windmill is fully functional, but it's not recording. We can see current real time images on the screen. That's all we have," Adam was explaining.

Liam rubbed his temples. That was checked quarterly. Something happened to the system, probably general wear and tear, since the last inspection. It did beg the question if Phillipe had anything to do with it because the timing was too perfect.

There was no tracking to use. Word from beneath the surface was that Phillipe had cut it out. Liam had suspected that from the beginning, but it had been a farfetched idea. It wouldn't be easy to do alone like Security suspected, and the thought of it made his skin crawl.

"There is one camera near the bank along the river between the windmill and the town," Adam said. "It was knocked down and has been recording brush for hours. This was noticed earlier, but with the alarm sounding, it hasn't been fixed."

"Any way to tell what happened to it?" Liam asked. Their cameras were securely hidden. If Phillipe had insider information as to where to find them, that could help significantly in determining who was aiding him.

"It was an animal. The images are blurry, but it looks like elk."

Liam groaned and stretched his neck. Phillipe was the luckiest son of a gun alive.

"We can tell, however," Adam went on, "that the elk had likely been scared off by bright green and yellow lights."

'The river! Phillipe had gone into the river, and the only person who would recognize him now was gone.'

"What about the edges of town?" Liam asked. "Do we have anything showing anyone who looks out of place? Their clothes? Being soaked? Anything that might set him apart?'

"We're still checking those," Adam said. "So far, we have nothing."

Liam ended the call and buried his face in his hands. No one had ever made it to the light of day until now, and it had happened on his watch.

The real question was why. There had been very few escape attempts because of how difficult it was, by all means it had been considered impossible until now, to accomplish. No one would dispute the conditions of the Below were subpar. Liam grew up there, and even if he hadn't, he would see it on the face of each new creature who made the transfer. There was the semi-permanent smile that didn't leave their faces for months. The way their eyes lit up over seeing every new and wondrous feature the surface offered never got old. In his years on the job, his favorite thing to witness was taking a new resident to the grocery store and explaining how, with rare exceptions, these options were always in stock at any time. They no longer had to make do with what the Below had managed to obtain, or what a business had prepared to sell that day.

It was both a literal and figurative night and day

difference between the two ways of life. No one would be faulted for wanting to come here, but they all knew the consequences. Well, they had an idea. The truth was far worse than they could imagine. The ones who had attempted an escape in the past were driven to it by some means. It was almost always family. Some poor creature who had been sent back and couldn't tolerate the downgrade coupled with their loved ones still on the surface, and it created an overwhelming need to return.

The sea nymph was a different story. She hadn't been playing with a full deck and tried to sneak out through the underwater tunnel systems. If it weren't for her incessant cackling as she went that echoed her location like a beacon, she might have made it. It happened long before tracking devices were invented and put to use. Her purpose for leaving was the claim the sailors had been calling to her.

But why Phillipe? Why now? He had no family. He had never lived on the surface, so he had no real connections aside from those who came through his office on their way up. Contact was virtually nil between the residents of the two worlds, and it went across the desk at one of the headquarter locations before reaching the addressee. Phillipe never corresponded with anyone on the surface. They needed to figure out his motivation before they lost him for good.

Chapter Twenty-Two

The Playground

The door at the end of the hallway near his classroom opened to a much smaller, private playground. They were in the old wing of the building, the original school house. This broken down, depressed looking play area had probably been a lot of fun to children when it was first laid out. Time had taken its toll on it. Most of the equipment was unsafe, and the scattered toys in the yard were more reminiscent of what an older child would discard when they grew bored with it or had rendered it useless for what its intended design had been.

Phillipe understood what it meant as soon as he saw it, but he hoped he was wrong. They couldn't be forced to use this forgotten part of the property for their break just because they were behind the other students. Even if they couldn't come outside at the same time, surely they'd be allowed to use the same area.

Mr. Donnelly announced, "Twenty minutes, class!" He was standing right next to his teacher, and his voice thundered which made Phillipe flinch.

The children ran off to what looked like their usual spots, in their regular groups to enjoy the little time they had outside of the classroom. Phillipe was disappointed to the point of feeling pained. He had been looking forward to seeing the kids he met yesterday. It had only been day one, but he knew he was making friends even though it was something he had never experienced before to recognize it for what it was, what it meant.

None of the children in his new classroom had attempted to get to know him yet. They hadn't introduced themselves at the end of the day yesterday or before class this morning. He spent lunch sitting alone, but not necessarily by himself. There wasn't enough room for him to be left at an empty table. The other boys at his table turned away from him to talk to the other kids. Any time he looked at someone preparing to break the ice, they gave him a judgmental look and quickly moved away.

He stood off to the side by himself for a few minutes, debating on what to do. There was a sandy area no one was using where he could play by himself, but that was all he had been used to at the orphanage. He didn't want to be lonely anymore. There were several groups of boys, and he tried to guess which one might be most accepting of him.

The one farthest away was the smallest. There were only three boys, two fauns and a cyclops. He felt like it was his best bet because they were outnumbered compared to the other groups.

Phillipe approached them slowly. One of the boys had devised a new game and was explaining how to play it to the other two. It sounded like it worked best when there were two teams of two, but they were going to figure out a way to do it with an odd number of players. He thought it was perfect. He could be their fourth. "Hey," he said, standing behind them.

None of them acknowledged him. He had spoken rather softly, so they likely didn't hear him.

He walked around until he was standing between and just behind two of the boys before he tried again. "Hey," he repeated, a little louder this time.

One of the boys, a troll named Magnus, turned to face him. "What do you want?" he sneered.

"Hi," he said, waving at the boys peering out from behind Magnus. "I'm Phillipe."

"What are you? A baby?" Magnus asked.

The words caught Phillipe off guard, and his head jerked back like he'd been slapped. The boys behind Magnus began to snicker, and it grew louder into a full rolling laugh.

"I didn't think they allowed babies in school," Magnus continued to the delight of his friends.

It took him a minute to swallow his emotions, so he could speak without his voice cracking. He didn't want them to hear how close he was to crying. They had never seen one of his kind. No one outside the orphanage had. "I'm a hydrohom-" he started to say.

"A baby!" Magnus shouted.

The other boys bent over, clutching their mid-sections. They were laughing loud enough now for everyone on the playground to hear them.

Phillipe looked around, and everyone was looking their way. Even Mr. Donnelly who stood next to the door like a guard keeping watch over his prisoners was staring directly at him.

Magnus and his buddies mimicked the cries of babies and rubbed at their eyes with their fists. "Boo hoo!" they shouted. "Look at the baby. The baby's gonna cry."

There were sounds of laughter from the whole playground. He lifted his head and saw them. The ones who weren't giggling and pointing his way were looking at him with disgust.

The sand was still open. None of them had made their way there yet. It was also near where Mr. Donnelly stood. If anyone treated him like this over there, his teacher would put an end to it. They might even get in trouble for being mean.

He walked over to it slowly and deliberately. He kept his head down, staring at the ground. Each step was controlled, so it wouldn't appear like he was running away. The eyes of all the children from his class seared his skin, and he felt his skin turning red from it. Every footstep felt awkward like he had suddenly forgotten how to do the simplest actions, and it worried him that his harassers could see his clumsy gait, giving them more fuel for their taunts. He took slow, deep breaths to keep the humiliation from rising and pouring out through his eyes.

When he reached the sand, he walked to the side and dropped to his knees. He didn't want to turn his back to everyone, but he didn't want to face them either. There were no toys nearby to play with and not much to do except sit and run his fingers through the grains which is what he did. Sometimes he found a small twig or rock, and he tossed them to the side in the grass near the sand.

It wasn't long until a shadow came near, growing larger until it completely engulfed him. He never lifted his head, not because he knew who it was, but because he was afraid he could be wrong. Mr. Donnelly's front hooves came into view, and Phillipe relaxed. The relief didn't last.

"Jacoby," Mr. Donnelly said.

He looked up at his teacher who was standing directly in front of him. "Yes, sir," he said, having learned yesterday after school this was how he wanted to be answered.

"There appears to have been some sort of incident involving you and other boys from the class."

It wasn't a question, and he wasn't sure if it was something Mr. Donnelly wanted him to explain. For that matter, he hadn't planned on reporting them. He didn't want to be known as a tattletale.

"It would seem there have been a number of problems caused by you since you joined my class, almost all of them not complying with the rules, and now, creating disturbances during play break. It's been less than twenty-four hours, Jacoby. I believe that's a record, making you the biggest trouble maker I've ever had the displeasure to teach."

Phillipe looked at him filled with surprised. It hadn't been his fault. He wasn't the one who had done anything wrong. He wanted to explain it, but struggled to find the words, any words at all. The shock he felt over what his teacher said was too strong. Finally, he managed to speak, but was interrupted before the first word was fully out of his mouth.

"I'm not interested in your excuses, Jacoby. Please note

my tolerance for those who rock the boat is nil, but my punishments are endless. This is your last warning."

Chapter Twenty-Three

Unwanted Guest

Things were going great. In fact, John was dumbfounded by just how remarkably well everything was playing out. He didn't know why Phillipe was here, and he didn't want to either. It had to be more than freedom. If it was merely a desperate attempt to flee the Below, he would've kept on going. The Guard doesn't exist everywhere, and Phillipe would know better than anyone else up top the cities where they were located, where their people lived.

The Guard would follow the trail if there was one to anywhere Phillipe headed, but eventually the search would be called off. The case would be closed. There were rumors in the Above that never reached beneath the surface. Even those who had been sent back never talked about them as far as John or anyone he knew from his old life was aware. They probably kept quiet from fear of what Security would do to them.

The only thing more powerful than fear was hope. The Authority didn't want anyone to have hope if they were plotting an escape. No one had successfully escaped the

Below, but once on the surface, it was a lot easier to escape the Guard.

When citizens made the move up, there were only a dozen or so large cities the Guard had headquarters in and monitored. These places were strategically chosen for their size and diversity making it seamless for people to blend.

But the Guard wasn't everywhere. There were cryptoids all across the globe who finally understood what it meant to have true freedom, to not have a tracking device logging your every move, to not need approval for any big changes in your life, and to not have to endure searches or interrogations every time one of your actions was questioned.

Phillipe had a different agenda, but he wasn't forthcoming about it. He had no family here, had no family at all. What he was doing in Rotterdam couldn't be good, and John hoped he accomplished whatever was so important he put his own life at risk to get here as quickly as possible. He wanted Phillipe to move on or get captured, so long as the role he played was never discovered.

It hadn't been all bad. Phillipe hadn't told Christine the real reason why he was here, only that he had escaped and would be moving on soon. There was nothing that could convince him Phillipe hadn't intentionally told his girlfriend the truth about him, about everything, but it did work in his favor.

Christine took the news extremely well. Like most humans, she had a passing curiosity about all things supernatural and mythical. Unlike most humans, learning of their existence didn't cause a panic. If anything, it brought them closer together because he didn't have to hide a part of himself anymore. No, it was more than that. For the first time, he could be himself instead of pretending this one small section of him was the whole deal.

He tried not to think about what would've happened if Christine had been a member of the majority. If she had not believed Phillipe, it might have turned out alright. He was thankful she didn't freak out over learning the truth because he believed Phillipe would stop at nothing to do whatever it was he was here to do. No one who managed to escape would allow a woman with anxiety over learning fictional beings live alongside her to be their downfall.

The road was paved for their future. There would be no more worry over how she was going to react. The concern now would be if she could be believable enough in how she responded when the Guard got involved. They didn't take kindly to cryptoids who already let the secret out to their loved ones, but most all of them did say something beforehand. Hopefully, she'd be a good enough actress the Guard didn't come down on him for it. It wasn't like blaming Phillipe would be a better defense.

'Phillipe.' The name was fast becoming a bad word in his vocabulary. It made him cringe whenever he heard someone else speak it. One day, he would draw the line that he never wanted to hear that name again, but for now, he had to do more than hear it.

His uninvited house guest had been there for three days, sleeping on the couch. It went without saying that Phillipe would have to be careful, not simply to avoid being caught, but to prevent John from being implicated in aiding and abetting. It might go without saying, but he still said it.

There was nothing unwavering in his threat to Phillipe. He would report him without a second thought if he didn't take every precaution.

Hindsight clarifies everything. John was so focused on how this could potentially affect him he never bothered to consider how good Phillipe had to be at staying undetected. He should've known anyone capable of making it to the surface without being caught would not easily be captured once here.

Phillipe slipped in and out of his small apartment so seamlessly John didn't notice. One moment they'd be in the kitchen and the next he'd be gone. Even when John locked the apartment down at night, he'd wake up in the morning to find Phillipe on the couch. He didn't have a key. Nothing had been broken or tampered with that John could see, but there he was, curled up, barely covering more than one cushion with his decreased height.

That was another unsettling area. Every time Phillipe reappeared, he looked like a completely different person. He'd barely stand above John's waist then take an hour long shower and emerge from the bathroom, towering over John with a squared jaw that added to his attractive looks. It was a feature that made John envious with his softer facial frame. There was every manner of height in-between as well. Each time it was a different distorted version of Phillipe, and it took a while to adjust.

He was there now, on the couch. John eyed him from time to time wondering if he could somehow see the transformation take place as he shrunk. It was too subtle to be visible in progress, but in the two hours since he woke, he could tell Phillipe was shorter than when he first saw him this morning.

They had survived two searches. The first was brief, but the second had been extreme. John stayed in the kitchen being interrogated by a member of the Guard. Of course, he insisted John wasn't a suspect, wasn't in any trouble, and it was all a formality, but it didn't feel that way. He felt like he was already on trial. During the long string of questions, two other Guard members combed his apartment. Everything was rummaged. No stone left unturned as they say. It took twice as long to clean the place after they left than it did for them to destroy it.

They survived both of the Guard's routine contacts. It should be smooth sailing for the rest of it as long as John isn't implicated. This is when he should be able to finally have a minute to relax before trying to figure out how to get rid of Phillipe. It should be calm for him after that, but nothing ever goes the way it should.

There was a loud knock at the door which terrified him until he remembered Christine was dropping by. They had plans for lunch which he had been hesitant to make, but he wanted to try to regain some of the normalcy in his life. He checked his watch. She was a little early, but that didn't matter. He was ready to go at any time.

John answered the door without hesitation, and without looking through the peephole. He was sure it was Christine. He pulled it open with a warm smile, saying, "Hey!"

The two men standing in the hall threw him into a panic. His heart stopped for seconds before pounding rapidly again to catch up then continued to increase in its rhythm. The flush that hit his face burned hot enough he believed they could not only see the red in his cheeks, but feel the heat from it as well. His mouth went dry, and he wasn't sure whether he should try to run past them or slam the door and lock it.

"Good morning, Mr. Reed," Simmons said. "You remember us? Simmons, and my partner Boyd," he said, nodding toward the other man. "Might we come in?"

Chapter Twenty-Four

Fact Vs Fiction

Phillipe ducked out the window as soon as he heard Simmons' voice. He'd been pretending to be asleep for a little while, waiting on John to leave. That man was too nervous, and it agitated him. If he was to finish what he set out to do, he had to remain calm. John didn't question him about his motives or even say much at all really, but it was the way he was always around like he wanted to know how long this would take without asking. He needed to back off.

The last time the Guard showed up unexpectedly, he was small enough to hide in the vents. He had done it because it was raining that day, and a man growing in size on the street is something people would definitely notice. It worked to his benefit because he heard everything being discussed.

Unfortunately, the Guard was on to the reason for his escape a lot faster than he expected. They didn't say much to John, but they asked him if he knew Brendan Roth. He'd have less time than he hoped, and it would be more difficult to complete his plan. The important thing was he knew. This time around, he didn't want to stay and eavesdrop. He needed to scout out Roth's home, see what kind of surveillance the Guard had on it.

He went to the corner of the small roof and pulled himself around to the window on the side of the building. The window wasn't from John's apartment, but he still had to be careful. He peeked inside and after seeing no one, he climbed over and down onto the platform under the window to reach the fire escape.

Once he was on the ground, he headed into a corner store to buy a bottle of water. The price of it was ridiculous to him, but it didn't matter. The only money he had was what he swiped from John shortly after he arrived. He walked down the street and headed into a parking lot, sitting on a block near the building about halfway through. He checked around carefully for cameras before sipping the water. Too much at once would bring unwanted attention from the lights that would shine. The dull glow emanating off his skin wouldn't be noticeable from the street in the broad daylight, and if anyone did see it, they'd chalk it up to a light reflecting from something nearby, one of the cars perhaps.

There were no recent photos of him anywhere. He made sure of it, but the Guard would take notice of any man less than average height. The only way to blend was to stay tall. He had to have patience as he continued to drink from the bottle slowly.

He took another sip and thought about Roth. When he was a child in the orphanage, he had asked about his parents constantly. He knew they were dead, but he wanted to know what happened to them. Each time he asked, he was told he wasn't old enough for that conversation, and sometimes, they'd admit they didn't know himself.

It was Mistress Dawly, of course, who finally told him the truth after he had his heart broken in high school. She'd spent more time than usual with Phillipe trying to cheer him up and finally asked if there was anything she could do. He told her he wanted to know about his parents.

The surprise she had over learning he hadn't been told yet seemed genuine. She didn't know what happened, but promised him she'd find out. Mistress Dawly always stayed true to her word.

He took another drink and shifted around on the parking block. The increase in size made it more difficult to fit between the block and the front of the car in the space.

It took a couple weeks, but she told him what she found out. He hadn't expected to cry. His parents were more like figments of his imagination instead of real people. He sobbed hard that night, thinking about what they went through, especially his mother. Mistress Dawly comforted him for as long as he needed.

His parents were trying to leave town. The Below had ordered an evacuation because it wasn't safe for their people any longer. Many creatures had been discovered and killed which set the whole town on edge looking for more. Mistress Dawly explained they had acquired passage on a boat and were boarding to start their lives over somewhere else.

As they boarded, his father somehow lost his balance and fell in the water. She didn't know if he had tripped, or if someone passed a little too close and knocked into him. Either way, he was an easy target once he was submerged. Men came from all around to help the sailors subdue him.

His father had fought back, trying to free himself, but he was killed.

The bottle was almost empty, so he finished it off. He was already at his full size, but he needed to wait a little longer before rushing off.

He was told his mom was arrested. Her fate, and the fate of the baby, were up in the air. Before anything could be decided, she went into labor and had died in childbirth. The magistrate devised a test to determine if Phillipe was non-human. He'd take the babe to the canal and hold him in the water. If he began to show any signs of transformation, he'd drop the babe, letting the water finish him off.

No one was aware of the water dragon who lurked nearby. As the magistrate was preparing to lower Phillips, she snatched him from the man's hands and brought him safely to the Below. He had always adored Kayda for this and still did. If she hadn't intervened, he probably wouldn't have lived through the night.

Almost every word of that story had been a lie. He didn't blame Mistress Dawly. She had passed away centuries ago, so he wasn't able to ask her about it anymore. He was certain she only passed on the information she had been told. It wasn't her lie that reached his ears; it was the Authority's.

Phillipe waited until he felt enough time had passed. Then he stood up and headed to the address he had memorized days ago. He used John's computer to map out a route while he was at the bakery a couple days ago. Actually, he memorized half the town just to be able to find his way to Roth's house from any direction.

It was time he set about what he had come here to do.

It was time to develop a plan of when and how was best to make his move. Roth's days were numbered, and he entertained himself with the various ways he could exact his revenge. There were three targets: Roth, his wife, and the child she carried. He didn't yet know how their lives would end, but he often contemplated whether or not vampires could float.

Chapter Twenty-Five

Phillipe's Friends

John glanced behind him at the couch without thinking, but it was empty. His eyes darted around the room, but he couldn't see Phillipe anywhere. The blanket that had been draped over him on the couch was now on the floor along with a book he asked John to check out at the library for him yesterday.

"Is someone with you?" Simmons asked, pushing the door open and barging inside.

"No," John said.

Boyd followed behind Simmons. "You seem nervous."

The two Guard detectives surveyed the room before bringing their attention back to John. Simmons motioned to Boyd to begin a search with his hands. "What's going on, John?" he asked.

"Nothing," he said. "I heard a noise, but it looks like the book I was reading fell," he added, glancing toward his living room.

Simmons nodded at him, but his face displayed his suspicions clearly. "We're sorry to intrude again, but it seems we may need you after all."

John had worried it would come to down to this. It would be near impossible to help the Guard and Phillipe simultaneously. The punishments he envisioned for helping Phillipe alone were all gruesome with the lightest being sent back down. If he tried to juggle both and was discovered, a death sentence would be avoidable, but the real fears lay in what he'd face before the compassion of death.

"We have a few leads," Simmons said, walking around the room inspecting a few items casually as he went.

"Oh, that's great news," John said, trying not to sound terrified. He was beginning to suspect they were there to arrest him and demand he give up Phillipe's whereabouts.

"Is it, John?" Simmons asked.

"Yes. I think everyone is ready for life to return to normal," he said.

Boyd joined them, shaking his head at his partner to indicate he found nothing during the search.

Simmons sighed and rested his hands on his hips. "You think that because you are unaware of the new information we have," he said.

That was the last thing John wanted to hear him say. He held his breath and waited for it. They had come to take him in for questioning. He'd never see his home or bakery again, and he wouldn't even be given the chance to say goodbye to Christine.

"It's been brought to our attention that Phillipe has friends on the surface," Boyd told him.

John tried to direct his attention to him while secretly watching Simmons who was inspecting various items in the living room. "You think someone may have helped him escape?" he asked.

"Possibly," Boyd said. "But we know he has friends here who would be willing to help hide him. Maybe help him in his next moves whatever they might be."

"Why do you think that?" he asked, waiting for the other shoe to drop.

"They told us," Simmons said.

John looked between the two of them in turn. His eyebrows furrowed, "They told you they were helping him?"

He couldn't imagine who *they* were, but the bafflement didn't end there. They weren't talking about him, couldn't be because he hadn't admitted a word. Yet, someone did, more than one someone. There were no circumstances in which he could dream of anyone owning up to anything freely. They had to be captured and forced to talk. His dilemma was steadily amplifying. If he didn't bring the truth to light, he would be responsible for their fate.

"Not exactly," Boyd said. "During the course of our investigation, we've spoken with a number of people who claimed they would do anything for him."

Simmons nodded. "Seems he made a lot of friends advising those who didn't think they stood a chance on how to pass their review to ascend."

With what he learned of Phillipe over the last three days, John didn't have him pegged as the type of guy to have many friends. It never occurred to him there might be others like him. People who were brought up their entire lives with the acceptance they'd never see the light of day until they had their meeting with Phillipe. He was good at what he did at the Authority.

"They insist they haven't seen him, of course, but would help him if he needed it," Boyd said. "We think they're being honest, on both points."

"There is one other name that's been on a lot of people's lips," Simmons added, stepping away to check out something that caught his eye.

Boyd came closer. "Do you know the name Geoffrey Edemez?" he asked.

"The name doesn't ring a bell," he said.

"Really?" Simmons asked, standing near the couch with his eyes squinted like he was studying it.

"Yeah, I mean I've met a few Jeff's, but I don't know their last name or anything. Maybe I've met him," John explained. His nerves were frazzled as he was getting the feeling neither detective believed him.

Simmons walked along the couch with his head tilted to the side, examining the area where Phillipe had been sleeping minutes earlier. It made John nervous, and he worried there was something there. Some clue left behind which would alert the detective to his house guest. "I find it hard to believe you aren't familiar with the djinn."

'*The djinn*,' John thought. He had met him once shortly after arriving, but others regaled him and his tales all the time. It is widely known he rarely stays put like the Guard demands, but travels to his heart's desire with the ability to come and go in a snap, returning from weeks of fun a few moments after he disappeared. "Mezzie," he finally said out loud.

"That's right. Edemez... Mezzie," Boyd said. "So you do

know him?"

"Not really," John said. "I met him once close to five years ago."

Boyd jotted something down in the little notebook he pulled from his pocket, and it worried John. Everything worried John. Phillipe needed to leave sooner than later. Simmons picked the book off the floor where it had fallen and was studying it carefully.

"It seems Mezzie has a deep appreciation for Jacoby," Boyd explained. "That's not uncommon. There are quite of few who feel they owe their freedom to him for helping them rise to the surface. But a djinn? That's a rare feat."

It was the source for many stories in the Below. Djinn's were real and had roamed the land freely thousands of years ago. Most of them long ago captured and trapped. Their whereabouts were still unknown, and everyone had a differing idea of how much, if anything, the Authority was doing to track them down like they claimed. Only one had ever been moved to the Below, and that was Mezzie.

Mezzie made it back to the surface over a thousand years before John had been born, but his was one of those rumors which had never died down. It was also the beginning of Phillipe's reputation as being the best case manager to ever grace the Authority halls. Some people saw him as a hero, while others insinuated there must be some form of sorcery to his methods, as it was the only logical explanation to how he moved some of the cryptoids to the surface.

The sound of Boyd's voice relaying how Mezzie had made numerous remarks over the years of his allegiance to Jacoby, vowing to do anything for him if it was needed, barely made it to John's ears. He was still in shock he hadn't made the prime suspect list yet.

"We want to question him," Boyd went on. "As you can imagine, bringing in a djinn isn't an easy task. That's where you come in."

John nodded. "Anything you need. What do you want me to do?"

Boyd's eyes lit up, but the smile never made it to his lips. "Happy to hear that John. Come with us down to the office, and we'll discuss our next move."

They headed to the door of the apartment, and Simmons held the book out to him before leaving. "This your book, John?"

"The library's actually, but yes," he half lied. John was the one who had checked it out at least.

"Interesting choice," he said, setting the copy of *Vampires: Myth vs Truth* on the copy table.

Chapter Twenty-Six

Empty Files

Maude thumbed the edges of the two files resting on her desk. It couldn't be put off forever. She'd have to make the trek up to Masterson's office showing him what she had found, but she dreaded it. This would be blamed on her. It would be her fault since she was the keeper of the records after all. It was her job to *keep* the records.

They fill you with pride in your work, telling you how important your role is to the company. They fill you with excitement about the future, telling you there are possibilities of promotion in a department consisting of one employee. They fill you with eagerness to do well, telling you they are open to any ideas you have to streamline, better organize, or improve the process. They fill you with lies, telling you what you want to hear before sending you off to collect a paycheck.

That was long before the electronic chips were utilized to track the files. Back then, it was part of her job to physically keep tabs on them. She'd spoke at a Security meeting not long after she began working there, explaining how easy it would be for information to go missing from the files or be copied for personal use. These files contained documentation that could easily be used to blackmail someone or worse. It would be worthwhile to search the files' content before and after being checked out, or better yet, create a room where the files could be looked over without actually leaving the records area. Yes, it was already an option, but they needed to make it a rule.

This was before Masterson came on board as head of security, and the old director wasn't interested in her opinions. He hadn't laughed, but she saw the humor in his eyes. "We'll deal with that *if* the time comes," he said.

Maude never mentioned it again and soon stopped sharing any ideas she had about overhauling the archives. No one wanted to listen to them anyway. Everyone felt like it was unnecessary because the punishments were enough to deter anyone from doing anything out of line. The Security office was too complacent to think they'd ever be challenged like this, and because of that, they were far too unprepared when Phillipe came along.

The Jacoby files were empty. Maude expected them to be the moment she received the phone call ordering her to bring them to Masterson's office. It wasn't because she suspected Phillipe of tampering with them. She would've reported it immediately if that were the case. It wasn't because she searched the logs and learned the only time Phillipe checked out anything from the archive room was when he needed background information to create a file for Meredith Jennings. The last names were close enough to give him unsuspected access to his parents' files. In fact, she didn't search the logs until after she discovered the empty files for herself.

It actually surprised her to find the file folders left behind. She didn't spend a lot of time wondering about the logistics of how he could manage to steal the files' content undetected, but it was obvious how he managed it after seeing the Jennings entry attached to his name. The reason she was certain he had found a way to these files was because he had done what no one else had ever accomplished. Phillipe Jacoby had escaped.

His name was fast becoming something close to legend in the Below. If he wasn't captured swiftly, he'd wind up a sort of folk hero to those who had no choice but to toll out their lives in this dingy hell. The rumors were already being whispered, and Below Security couldn't stop that from happening just like they couldn't track down the source of the leaks. Everyone had heard about Phillipe's daring escape. More importantly, they knew he made it. Honestly, she secretly rooted for Phillipe even though his actions put her job at risk.

If Maude didn't head upstairs soon, she'd have Masterson after her because he needed these files. They wouldn't help him, and they would only serve to put the blame on her. The archives were her responsibility, and it wouldn't matter she had followed protocol to the letter where Jacoby was concerned. It wouldn't matter she had proposed changes which would've prevented this before Masterson's parents had been born. It would be mentioned why she hadn't continued to speak up about ways to improve their system, but really it would come down to this being her department.

She sighed heavily and rolled her head around with her eyes closed. It was time to face the music. Better to get it done and over with then wait for Masterson's anger to grow.

It was four stories to the main floor of the Authority building. Maude could run up the stairs with ease. The legs of a faun were built for this type of exercise. She was in no hurry today, taking the steps one at a time slowly, but without trying to add unnecessary stalling to her trek.

Once on the ground floor, she tucked the files under one arm as she walked down the main hallway with the file names facing inward. If anyone saw the files and read the names on them, she'd be stopped and questioned about it. Not right away of course. No one would dream about it while at the Authority, but the word would spread easily. There'd be no peace when she left for the day. People would stop her on the street and maybe show up uninvited at her home to press her for details. She'd rather stay out of the gossip on the spreading end, but had no qualms being on the receiving end of it.

Masterson's office was on this floor, but he wasn't there. She had been instructed to bring the files to the Security floor two flights up. The staircase was halfway down the main hall. From the main floor, there were two different sets of stairs. One for the main offices that went from the ground floor up, and the other to storage and archives from the ground floor down. No one really understood why the two couldn't be connected.

There was no one around which was odd. The hall was typically abuzz with employees headed here or there, talking each other up about some random subject, or just trying to avoid their actual work load. It was empty and eerily quiet. Either everyone had been given special tasks in light of the escape, or they were hiding from Masterson, hoping to avoid his wrath from being in the wrong place at the wrong time. Both were valid options.

Maude continued to take careful, deliberate steps. Her mind raced with a variety of possible fates she was about to meet from accusations, to yelling, blame placing, and even termination. Yelling was a certainty regardless of the rest. She tried to prepare for it by having her defense ready, but she was blindsided when she walked through the Security office doors.

Masterson was standing at the end of a long conference table surrounded by a couple Security members, being updated and looking at paperwork. The atmosphere change in the room was like stepping into a different world. There was a constant hum of chatter as orders were given, questions asked and answered. A constant stream of employees made their way in and out of the main office into their private offices in the back or wherever it was they were headed.

When he noticed her, Masterson asked, "The files were empty, weren't they?"

Chapter Twenty-Seven

First Love

Phillipe was counting down the days until the end of his sixth year. There was only one more to go after this, and he couldn't wait to put all of it behind him. This school had done nothing for him in all the years he'd been here. Mr. Donnelly's treatment of him never bettered either. It made no difference how well he excelled. He had proven time and again he was the smartest in the class, well qualified to study with the main population of the school, but he remained sectioned off, treated as less than the rest.

It didn't end with his classroom. The orphanage was far too restrictive for someone coming of age, and he yearned for the day when his freedom was at hand. Everyone told him to enjoy these days when there were no responsibilities. They told him once the real world hit he'd miss the days of his youth, but Phillipe wagered it was untrue, at least for him. There was nothing about his miserable, pathetic life to date he could imagine ever reminiscing over.

Then there was Emilia. They were limited in their time together. The orphanage made a few allowances for him out of pity, but he was still run by a stricter hand than anyone else his age. Whenever he had a moment of freedom, they'd steal away to somewhere secluded and enjoy the precious little time they had together.

Of all the women in the Below, she was one of a select few who might provide him a chance for a future. Everyone here was a cryptid mutation, but those genetic differences, which once had a close direct link to each other, had been evolving almost since the dawn of time. Many of them appeared no different from humans and could pass as relatives, but in reality, they were as different as fish and birds.

All of the species in the Below cared about their bloodlines. There was a unified, albeit almost desperate, belief they would one day return to the surface to roam as freely as their ancestors had done. Humans would not last. Their wars, waste, and whole hearted hatred of anything they perceived as a threat would be their undoing. Every cryptoid followed the news of their destruction with baited anticipation for when they could return. Most of them knew it wouldn't be in their lifetime, but they all held the same goal of having a descendant rise to the top.

It was this belief more than anything else behind the discrimination of interspecies relationships. Flings and affairs were often overlooked in youth, but it wasn't allowed to become more than that. Bearing children was a priority.

This is the reason Phillipe felt he found a mate with Emilia. Lamias possessed a trait a relative few species throughout history could boast. Females could reproduce without a male counterpart. It could occur either way, but in the event there was no suitable mate, the female could lay fertilized eggs on her own.

Phillipe didn't learn this until long after he had fallen for her, and it was the best news – no, the only good news he had ever received. There actually was someone he'd be able to have by his side for life. That was a bit of a stretch as he was immortal, but lamias lifespans had been known to exceed five hundred years which he felt was as close as he would come.

They still had to keep their relationship a secret. Emilia wasn't allowed to date until after her schooling was finished. Her father would be furious and would prevent them from seeing each other again until after graduation. It was only for another year. Then everything opened up for them. They could take their relationship public, and he'd no longer be under the shadow of the orphanage. The world would be theirs. Well, the part of the world that lied under the surface anyway because like him, lamias could never blend in up top.

The easiest way for them to meet up was for her to lie and say she was with friends. Phillipe could get free time away a couple times a week now that he was older, but it wasn't guaranteed. When he was denied, he suffered a gauntlet of emotions all night because he had no way to get word to Emilia. Luckily, it didn't happen often, and she learned to wait until they saw each other outside of the school building the next day before assuming the worst.

There was a market about halfway between them where they could easily get lost in the crowd. It was a little farther for Emilia, but it worked. They'd meet up and head off to one of their hideouts. The place they chose depended on how much time they had and what their plans were for the night.

Tonight, they headed to their make out spot behind the school house. It wasn't well lit at night, and they could hide behind the building because the back of the property had a high fence around it. The lock on the front gate was broken. It had been for as long as Phillipe could remember, but no one had ever made it a priority to fix it which served to their benefit. As long as they made sure the street was empty before slipping onto the school property, they were in the clear.

Once around back, they sat in their usual place along the fence. It gave them a good view of the front of the school. In the darkness, they wouldn't be able to see much more than shadows, but it was better than nothing if someone else came along. They'd sit and talk for a little while, making plans for their life together once they were free.

Phillipe didn't mind the chit chat, but he couldn't wait to have her in his arms again. She was much longer than he was even at his full height, but she'd coil up to be as comparable to him as she could. After they started making out, all thoughts of keeping an eye out in case someone appeared were lost. No one else had ever come the entire time they had been sneaking onto school grounds. They felt safe there. They let their guard down. Even if someone did come along, they would probably be there to hide what they were doing too, which meant they'd have no desire to rat the two of them out. Neither of them expected what was about to happen.

"Get your hands off my daughter!" a voice hissed.

Emilia's father slithered closer, towering over both of them.

They scrambled to their feet. Luckily, they had only just arrived and not a single article of clothing had been removed yet. As soon as he was upright, Emilia's father swung his tail, knocking Phillipe to the ground and pinning him with it. "If I ever see you near my daughter again, it will be the last time anyone sees you," he threatened. "Are we understood?"

Phillipe nodded as he tried to push the tail away. It was heavy for his small size and made it difficult to breathe.

Emilia pleaded with her father nothing had happened, not really. She begged him to be lenient, insisting Phillipe was a great guy.

"We'll have plenty of time to talk about this at home," he said. "You're grounded." His tail whacked across Phillipe one more time before they left.

Phillipe lay there for a long time, coughing and clutching his abdomen. In the darkness, he wouldn't be able to see the marks under his shirt, but they were there. Most of his torso was bruised, and he would later discover two of his ribs were broken. The physical pain hurt, but it was nothing compared to the idea of not being able to see Emilia.

Chapter Twenty-Eight

Serena

John sat in the backseat of Simmons' car feeling more like someone under arrest than a person helping the Guard with their investigation. After their initial explanation back at the office of what they had planned, no one said much which barely helped to set him at ease. His heart raced, and he worried it had all been a trick.

The Guard knew he'd been harboring Phillipe. They weren't going to Roth's house for him to meet the couple and study the layout of the home in case the Guard had reason to send him there later. He was being taken to one of the Guard prison locations where he would be held. John didn't know for how long, but it would end with him being sent back Below. As the car moved through the city, his thoughts of what he feared awaited him grew.

The beat of his heart echoed in his ears, and he wished Simmons or his partner Boyd would crank the radio to drown it out. It was a beautiful day, and they had the windows cracked which allowed various sounds from the street to seep inside the car. It was the only thing preventing them from hearing how loud his heart was thumping. If he didn't regulate himself and fast, it wouldn't be long before it was louder than the white noise.

Beads of sweat formed along his brows, but he was too anxious to wipe it away for fear of drawing attention to himself, to how nervous he was. When they questioned him about it, and they would, he'd say it was the heat. It wasn't too uncomfortable in the car, but it was warmer than he preferred. He'd blame it on the lack of air conditioning.

The car slowed to a stop in a residential neighborhood which offered a brief moment of hope. The Guard was notorious for their secrecy. They had to be. When he was back home in his apartment, he'd breathe a sigh of relief, but not one second before then. It would be short lived too because his next steps were to figure out how to rid himself of Phillipe.

They got out of the car, and John looked around, wondering which house belonged to a vampire. This would be his first time meeting one. There were a handful or so in the Below, but he never had any interactions with them. He definitely didn't think there were any on the surface in this age.

"Ready?" Simmons asked.

John only nodded. He was too afraid he'd give away his guilt ridden nervousness if he tried to speak.

Boyd laughed, and said, "That's not too convincing."

Simmons walked up to John. "Hey, there's nothing to fret here. We've got eyes all over the neighborhood. We just want you to meet the person you're helping. That's it."

He took a deep breath and cracked his neck. "Let's do

this."

John had a thousand reservations running through his mind when he arrived at Brendan Roth's house. He was worried he'd be found out by the Guard. There was a little excitement over meeting a vampire, but if everything he'd ever heard about them were true, Brendan would be able to detect exactly how nervous and scared he was. All of these thoughts dissipated the moment he met Serena.

The first thing he noticed was her beauty. It was like someone from the pages of a magazine had come to life. Then she smiled. It was friendly and so warm it could melt the problems of the entire world. Everything about her was flawless. Each strand of hair was perfectly in place to achieve what was considered a messy look, and her makeup could've easily been done by a team of professionals. Even the way she walked commanded attention. When she laughed, it was a symphony playing in his ears. None of this is what he would remember about her when he left with the detectives a short time later.

Serena was pregnant. There was no mistaking the rounded protruding midsection on her slender frame for anything else. Not only was she pregnant, but this baby wasn't long from making an appearance. A vampire had found a human companion with the ability to bear him a child.

This couple was Phillipe's target, or the Guard believed so anyway. It wasn't simply an escape to reach the Above which he'd always suspected, but it had been confirmed that morning. John didn't understand how a vampire who had been on the surface longer than Phillipe had been alive could have managed to trigger his rage to this extreme, but he was confident the Guard wouldn't be protecting them without good cause.

He wanted to confess. From the moment he saw Serena, he wanted to lay it all out in the open. It might be why the Guard brought him here first before tracking down Mezzie. If they suspected John had any information on Phillipe, introducing him to the target may sway his tongue to talk. It almost worked, but he had to think about Christine. He couldn't risk Phillipe getting to her before he was captured, and he couldn't bear to break her heart when he was sent to the Below for his part in hiding Phillipe.

There had to be another way. He could play both sides of this. With Phillipe in his apartment, he could find out as much as he could and use it to help the Guard find him without either of them being wise to what he was doing. It was worth giving it a shot before coming clean about everything. One way or another, he had to prevent anything from happening to Serena even if it meant sacrificing his freedom to do it.

"Hello, John. It's a pleasure to meet you," Serena said, after everyone was seated in the front room. "I've heard so much about you."

John cocked his head to the side and wondered if it was possible her husband had been forthcoming with her. Brendan is supposed to keep secrets of other cryptoids to himself. It goes without saying he will tell his wife everything. It's the spouse privilege. Still, she isn't *supposed* to know which could land her husband in trouble after the dust settles from Phillipe's capture.

"We've met with her and discussed how you could help," Simmons said. "What with your specific attributes and all."

'Of course they did,' he thought, not realizing how his stress was affecting his ability to think straight. He rubbed the back of his head and looked at the coffee table, finding it difficult to make eye contact with Serena. She would've never heard the name Phillipe Jacoby if John had turned him in from the start. "How do you want to do this then?" he asked. "Are you going to leave me here?"

Chapter Twenty-Nine

Scouting Exits

Masterson sat at his desk with his head in his hands. It had been over forty-eight hours since Jacoby breeched the surface. The Guard was nowhere near close to finding him. Chances were he wasn't even in Rotterdam any longer, and if it weren't for Roth, that's exactly what he'd believe.

He lifted his head and sighed, looking at the map of the world on the wall across his office. It had been a gift from a former Security member who transitioned years ago. Shortly after arriving in the Above, he sent it down for Masterson. If you want to call it a gift, that is. It's a hell of a way to say thanks by sending a map filled with every place the recipient will never be able to visit.

Unsure whether the fellow meant well by it or was simply rubbing in Masterson's face all the places he'd never see, he had hung it on his wall, taking it in stride either way. He leaned back and crossed his arms, staring at it with his head cocked to the side. The map had garnered more attention in the last two days than in all the years since he'd received it. Most of the time he forgot it was there.

Without realizing what he was doing, he lifted one hand to his mouth and bit gently on the tips of his fingers. It was how he broke his nail biting habit in his youth, but it resurfaced sometimes when he was under a lot of stress. He stared at the map, hoping for some glimmer or sparkle, some speck of magic to point the way, telling him Jacoby was indeed still in Rotterdam. He wanted a sign indicating the clues pointing to Roth weren't a red herring, or he hadn't fled temporarily, waiting for surveillance to relax before he made his move. Maybe the freedom of the Above was enough to curb his lust for revenge, and he had a change of heart. No, he didn't imagine that was the case at all.

The magical answer he was hoping for wouldn't come. It had been banned in the Below almost as soon as this refuge had been established. By all means, it wasn't merely outlawed. An invisible barrier had been put in place by a sorcerer who was celebrated for knowingly curbing his own abilities for the greater good. He was arrested two days later when it was discovered he manipulated the barrier in a way to exclude himself. They exercised extreme caution when jailing him to keep his hands bound and his mouth stifled to prevent Ambrose from using magic to free himself. It worked a little too well. Without magic keeping him eternally young, he withered and passed away before judgement could be served. Many feared his death would break the spell, but it had not. Ambrose had listened to the Authority and secured the magic even in the wake of his demise.

Ambrose cast the spell which meant Ambrose was the

only one who could undo it. There would be no magic aiding the detectives on the case unless they willfully, and in the long run regrettably brought a magic wielding creature to the surface. Although many had never been rounded up to come to the Below when it was created, very few had ever been allowed to make the move back. None had ascended since Mezzie. The ones who existed on the surface were untraceable. Their magic prevented the Guard's control, and no one trusted putting anyone with such abilities into a secure position as they'd likely use it to their own means. This case, as with all cases, had to be solved the old fashioned way.

A knock on the door interrupted Masterson from his wishful thinking. "Come in," he said, trying to retain his usual commanding tone, but he failed. His voice sounded as weak as his hopes for apprehending Jacoby.

The door opened and a sheepish Gordy walked in the office. "Sir," he said.

Masterson took a deep breath and straightened up in his chair. "What do you have for me?"

Gordy shifted nervously and opened his mouth to speak before composing himself and walking to the desk. "We've been checking the tapes," he said.

"And?" Masterson asked, reaching for the tablet Gordy was carrying.

He shifted his gaze away from his boss, praying Masterson understood the phrase don't shoot the messenger. "Jacoby's been planning this for years."

Masterson played the video displayed on the screen. Clips of footage began playing in a montage. Each was the same and entirely different. Jacoby was in frame on each piece of video, walking through the Below. Only he wasn't walking through the underground city, but rather, walking the outskirts, near the edges of town. Mostly he stuck to the main roads and paths that would around, staying away from the barren lands that surrounded the Below.

As the videos continued to play, one after another, there were a few where he neared the edge as close as he could manage. In some he was confronted by Security on post at tunnel entrances or making their rounds, but at other times, they acknowledged each other in a friendly manner. They had grown accustomed to seeing Jacoby taking late night strolls in areas where he had no business to be. Doing what? Did they really believe he simply couldn't sleep, so he decided to walk two miles from home to tire himself? Or he was getting his exercise in the middle of the night?

The time stamps on the videos ranged from when he left his job to shortly before when the Security office began lighting their world for the day. From what he was seeing, Jacoby never walked the same exact route twice. Masterson touched the tablet face, pausing the video. The red tracking bar at the bottom was a blip on the left side of the screen. There were hours of footage in this one compilation to comb through.

"Let me guess," Masterson said with a sigh. "These strange habits of his were never reported?" There was too much comfort in the routine of all who dwelled beneath the surface. Even their crime rate was almost nil, providing a sense of ease and peace that was taken for granted. The rare escape attempts of the past were few and far between, and those had all been spontaneous. A sliver of an opportunity presented itself, so someone jumped at the chance. Another might have received devastating news and tried to break free. No one had been dumb enough to plan an escape before, but in Jacoby's case, it was more accurate to say no one had been intelligent and capable enough to pull it off.

"They were documented," Gordy said. "At least, the earlier ones had been."

"Earlier ones?" Masterson asked, looking up from the paused image of Jacoby walking along the stream that had been carefully dug out to border one side of the city.

"Yes, well, after some of the team got to know him, they stopped writing it up in their shift reports, saying it was just Jacoby, and they didn't believe he was causing any harm."

"And what about now?" Masterson asked. "Do they still believe he was merely taking a stroll?"

Gordy looked at his feet and shifted his weight. "No, sir. They realize he was scouting out the best exit."

Chapter Thirty

Creating Distractions

Mezzie delighted in his ability to transport anywhere at a whim. The ability had been blocked in the Below. The barrier created by Ambrose didn't have a full effect on djinn's although the test pool consisted only of himself. His powers to create were as strong there as on the surface because his weren't based in magic. It did prevent him from whisking away to the surface on his own which he still couldn't understand unless Ambrose worded his spell to include all creatures, but that couldn't be since residents were given the approval to move up regularly. It hurt his head to think about it, so he tried to avoid it whenever the thought popped into his mind. And, it had been on his mind a lot lately.

That was the reason for more frequent than usual pub stops. Ever since the news of Phillipe reached his ears, he wondered how he did it. If a djinn like Mezzie couldn't escape the fortress the Below hailed as a safe house for all unique creatures, how in the world did Phillipe pull it off?

He'd buy Phillipe a drink if he saw him. It was impressive

what he managed to accomplish, and Mezzie was proud, not only of his escape, but regarded Phillipe's utter contempt for all the Below stood for as heroic. More should take notice and strive to repeat his actions. He'd have a drink with him then transport him anywhere to avoid capture, but Phillipe couldn't be found.

Word got around their small, widespread, but tight community fast. The Guard was searching for him, assuming he was involved since there were no leads yet on Phillipe's location. "Good luck to them," Mezzie muttered, lifting his glass. "They'll need it."

He walked out the door of the small bar and was blinded by the sun. It was easy to forget how early the day was while crammed in a darkened room soaked with the smell of alcohol and little whiffs carried over from last night's festivities where patrons didn't make it to the bathroom in time. The sand sprawled out in front of him, and it was nearly empty. Even for the off season, it was rare to see only a scattering of people lounging on the beach which meant it must be earlier than he thought.

As he walked to the small house he'd been renting for two months, he wondered what he should do. His work here wasn't done. It wouldn't be finished until he located and freed Thalia. She was the last of his kind captured and would be the best aide in finding the rest. If anyone held any secrets to where they were, it was her.

The house was no more than a shack by comparison to how he was used to living although it was fairly standard for the area. It was one room with the bed near the door and a small icebox in the back. Bathrooms were considered optional in these parts, but there was a community shower down the street. Neither bothered him much. He'd spin off to the finest hotels and use an empty room whenever it was necessary.

"Blaach!" Mezzie covered his mouth and nose with his hand to stifle the gag from the smell of the home. The stench of the former tenants saturated everything including the dirt floor. Nothing could remove the stench of human waste and decay.

He grabbed what he needed and headed outside in the fresh air as quickly as possible, weighing his options. In his pocket was the stone, half of it, and he fumbled it around with his fingers as he thought things over. There was time. He already had the first piece and recently learned the location of the second half. If no one had found the sorcerer's tsavorite yet, then no one was looking for it. At the time it was split, the halves may have been hidden well, but time eased the memory of the stone's power. The two halves had surfaced many times, making it easy for Mezzie to track.

The harder task was locating his kind which was why he needed Thalia. It had been centuries since she was imprisoned. She would never have to know he made her wait a little longer.

Phillipe hadn't asked for his help. Any creature who had crawled to the surface were able to contact him. All he had to do was ask. Mezzie could continue his work until then. "It's more than that, isn't it?" he asked himself under his breath.

'*It's decided then,*' he thought. He would head to Rotterdam at once to be at the ready if Phillipe needed him. In the meantime, his presence alone could provide more assistance to the odd loner who was short in stature. Mezzie's presence would attract the attention of the Guard who had been searching for him since the day they released him into the world, thinking he would actually follow their rules. The Above isn't freedom when your life is still under the control of the Authority.

If he's in Rotterdam, the Guard will be convinced he's there to aide Phillipe. The attention will be on him, giving the man he owed his freedom room to breathe and perhaps enough cover to make a clean getaway. It was the least he could do for him.

Mezzie wandered through the streets, barely better than dirt roads. They hadn't been formed by anything more than the foot traffic of those who lived there. Children were everywhere, playing and begging, approaching him for something he may have stashed in his pockets. They had all seen him before and recognized him as a generous man who always had a treat or a coin. He didn't want to be detained today at the risk of upsetting them and feeling the small stones they threw after him pepper along his back. *'It wasn't good for the children to be so expectant of others,'* he thought. It's a life lesson they need to learn.

There had to be a quiet spot where he wouldn't be noticed when he left. Going back to his shack was out. The mere thought of the smell residing within made him gag. The use of his abilities needed to be scarce to prevent the Guard from tracking him. Once he animated somewhere, the Guard would descend upon him, but he would be long gone before they arrived. He never surfaced at his true desired location. This time he would. He would arrive in

Rotterdam to help his old friend.

He finally came across an area seemingly deserted and waited to be sure before leaving. After a few minutes, he scoured once more, but missed the set of eyes intently watching his every move. There was a contained flash of light, and he was gone. The unknown observer hurried to the spot, collecting the residue of the djinn's powers to study.

Chapter Thirty-One

Emilia's Absence

Phillipe waited outside the school the next morning, frantically searching the students as they arrived waiting to see Emilia's beautiful face. She never arrived. He was always one of the first ones at the school due to the schedule the orphanage kept for him, and there was usually about a ten minute wait before Emilia showed up. The ten minutes came and went while Phillipe began to worry.

Her father was strict and had a temper. Emilia never mentioned suffering any abuse at home, but Phillipe wouldn't be assured she was alright until he saw her, talked to her, heard it from her. He paced near the entrance, not wanting her father to see him waiting at the gate after last night, but he kept the gate in sight at all times to avoid missing her. Not that he could. Her stature towered over almost all the other students. Her presence was still large even when coiled.

Had he missed any signs? Did he listen to her? Really listen? He'd been so focused on how he felt about her, how he felt about himself when he was with her, he failed to pay attention to the things she didn't say. Try as he may to replay all their conversations in his head, he was coming up empty on the important bits.

He vowed he'd be a better listener from this point forward. When he was with her, it'd be less about him. Emilia deserved to be with someone who understood her, who knew her every little detail, flaws and all. From now on, he would be the man she deserved instead of idly being content with her being perfect for him. He'd never again have to wonder what she may be going through and if she needed him.

The minutes continued to tick by without Emilia. Phillipe wrestled the urge to leave, to go to her house, to demand to see her. He had to find out if she was in any danger. Any father would be angry to catch their daughter in such a compromising position. Add to it the lies she told to be with him when she wasn't allowed to date in the first place, not to mention who he was. Most of those in the Below saw him as second rate. The last of his kind who would soon be extinct with no means to save the species. They wrote him off as nothing and had done so since Kayda delivered him to the waterway entrance of the Authority building so many years ago. It was a recipe for disaster, and the blood drained from Phillipe's face as thoughts of what her father could have done to her raced through his imagination.

Phillipe jumped when the school bell was rung, and several students nearby snickered, muttering to each other how weird he was. It was a split second decision. If he was going to leave, head to her house, and possibly confront her father, he'd have to do it now. He turned and walked into the building instead with his head hanging low. His side still pained with every step. He was no match for him, not at this size, and perhaps not at any size. There wasn't much he would accomplish by going there except creating more trouble for Emilia and placing himself in the hot seat, both at school and the orphanage.

The seconds ticked by in a slow, agony filled rhythm. Mr. Donnelly's lectures were typically boring and dragged out each class period, leaving little time to do the examples he assigned. Even when he finished with Phillipe's level, the sound of his voice lecturing other students made it virtually impossible to concentrate. School days lasted forever, and the evenings raced by in a blur. Today was worse. Time stood still while he waited for classes to end for the day, the earliest he could see if Emilia had ever made it to the building.

Donnelly's thundering voice echoed in his ears, but he didn't understand a word his teacher said. The work in front of him was as foreign as the chirps and squabbles the pixies hummed to each other in the marketplace. It would be a tedious night at the orphanage finishing his examples while answering questions from the mistresses who wondered why he suddenly had so much to work on outside of school.

His pencil fell to the floor and he bent over in his seat to grab it. The desk he used was only a desk in the loosest definition of the word. It was half a table found broken in storage, held up by a cheaply made wooden support with a stool for him to sit. Someone had found it and set it up in the room after his first day in the classroom for the unwanted, but as years passed, more desks opened. Mr. Donnelly wouldn't let him switch seats, wouldn't allow him the comfort of an actual desk or even a table he didn't have to constantly balance during the day to avoid a crash.

As he bent underneath it, he noticed the split piece of wood. It hadn't always been like that. *'Or had it?'* Maybe the support had been damaged too, and that's why it was spared for someone as insignificant as everyone viewed him to be. He reached out and touched the part angling toward him, jagged and sharp like a dagger waiting to hit its mark.

"Ouch," he muttered under his breath, yanking his hand back hard enough to bang it on the underside of the table.

Mr. Donnelly's voice silenced, and Phillipe looked up at him to see his teacher glaring at him. The teacher's left eyebrow slowly raised in an arch seeming to reach halfway to his hairline, and his lips pursed together. Phillipe didn't say a word. He wasn't green to this challenge. To speak would guarantee a mark by his name, and those marks came too easily without merit for him to intentionally risk punishment by all those who held control over his life.

'Not for much longer.'

He kept his eyes straight ahead, focused on the book his teacher had tucked inside the sash he wore at the base of his shirt where his torso met his chestnut hair covered body. In his hand, he held the pencil to the paper as if ready to work on his penmanship, copying the passage from his book as Donnelly assigned. If his eyes shifted in the slightest, his teacher may choose to give him a mark for being insolent.

'Not today.' Phillipe swallowed, and it gulped down his gullet harsher than he'd hoped. *'Today, I win.'*

His teacher began speaking a full minute before tearing

his eyes away to the group of students he was lecturing. Phillipe dropped his eyes to his paper and spun his pencil around, imitating the act of writing.

'Emilia might be in trouble.' The thought kept coming back to him, breaking his concentration which is why he gave up trying to focus on his work altogether.

'She needs you.' His inner voice took a more direct route to action.

Phillipe dropped his hands to his lap and allowed his pencil to roll off his leg, hitting the floor once more. Donnelly turned and came for him. The snort from his teacher was one of the few qualities of a horse his upper half mimicked. Phillipe reached for the pencil quickly before his teacher made it to his desk, and as he sat up, he slammed his hand into the sharpened splintered piece of wood.

Chapter Thirty-Two

This Is Now

Phillipe found Brendan easily enough. Of course, a thousand years ago his name would've been Brendis Roth. Luckily, the Authority office kept accurate, up to date tabs on all of the creatures they sent to the surface. Brendan's address was handed to him on a silver platter. All he had to do was look it up.

There was a record of every keystroke he had ever made on his work computer. He had to act fast. It was only a matter of time before Security checked his work history to see what he had been up to. They would find the digital files that he didn't have reason to access. Confidentiality was a strong suit at the Authority office. Snooping into others' files without authorization was grounds for immediate termination, but Phillipe was long past being fired.

It wouldn't take long for Security to find what they were looking for on his computer. There was only one odd man out. In his entire work history of multiple centuries of servitude to the Authority, there was one single file he had searched without permission. It was for the sole purpose of locating this vampire.

Phillipe chuckled, *'There had to be a better name for them than that.'* The word was outdated now.

He moved away from the front window of the tiny home across the street from where Brendan lived with his newest wife. She was Roth's new pregnant wife to be more specific. He walked through the house checking the back door was unlocked for at least the seventh time. He had no idea who lived here, or when to expect anyone to return home. His escape route had to be clear.

Returning to the front windows, he watched and waited. There was a car in the driveway, but he couldn't be sure Brendan was the one at home. He was only going to get one chance at this. It would do no good to show his hand too soon.

The Guard had already began sweeping through an initial search of all the creatures' homes. John Reed had been one of the first. Phillipe hadn't been present for it, but John had been smart enough to keep his mouth shut. A poor sap in love is likely to do anything to keep his sweetheart safe.

Once they finish their routine search and come up empty handed, the Guard would increase their tactics. That's not entirely true. They would intensify during a second search, but it was already a full blown investigation. They would be checking all the surveillance cameras they had access to and hacking into the ones they didn't. No one knew what he looked like at this height, but it wouldn't take long before the footage revealed the stranger who stumbled into town from the woods around the time of his escape. It would be shocking if they hadn't already discovered him and had his current picture sent out through their emergency contact system to all of the legendary creatures, Above and Below.

'Vampire though?' he thought to himself. At one time, a new creature was discovered, or mutated, or whatever happened to bring them into known existence. They had been around long before the Below Authority had been created. The species needed a name, and someone, somewhere thought vampire had a nice ring to it. It wasn't bad really as far as species' names went. Try saying hydrohomunculus three times fast.

Then the true nature of the vampire was discovered by humans, and they did what humans do best. They exaggerated and lied. As each of them retold the tale of an experience with this creature, they added a new and different spin to make the vampire seem more menacing and frightful. Something to be feared. Something to be killed.

'The movie makers of the twentieth century came along and turned the stories into a bat like human shape shifter. Their version of the vampire was so grotesque and so demonic it gave children, and even some grown adults, nightmares. Recent years had turned it into something even more disgusting: a heartthrob.

It wasn't long until the new definition of vampire in no way matched the creatures that bore its name. It's true they did have immortality. It was also true they do drink human blood, but they prefer it in a glass. They had never attacked humans with fangs bared, ripping through the flesh of the throat as the legends state.

The Guard delivers bags of freshly donated blood sourced from a contact at a local blood bank whenever it's needed. It's how they return to their youthful good looks when the passing of time takes its toll. It's an elixir for all that ails them, including old age. The way to kill them stayed constant. Their head had to be severed. The brain could not heal what it could not control.

The sound of an approaching car caught Phillipe's attention. He carefully peered out the window to avoid being seen. His breathing shallowed, and his heartbeat raced. It could be the returning owner of the home he was borrowing, but he wanted it to be Roth arriving home. He wanted it so desperately he tried to will it into reality. The car continued past, not stopping at either house.

Phillipe stared at the SUV sitting in the driveway of Roth's home and wished it could somehow tell him Roth's location. It wasn't the one on file for Roth at the Authority office, but that really didn't mean a thing. It could be a rental or belong to a friend or family member. Even if it was the one on record for him, it would not guarantee Roth was home. He needed to visually see him in his residence before he could make a move. That meant he had to either see Roth enter the home, or he would have to wait for the cover of darkness to venture closer.

The front door across the street opened, and Phillipe sucked in his breath. This is what he feared would happen. Roth had been home the entire time. He could have made his move, but now it was too late. He wasn't sure how many chances he would get. It would be anyone's guess how long it would be before another opportunity came along, and time wasn't on his side.

It wasn't Roth. Two men stepped outside and carefully

surveyed the street. They were dressed in plain clothes just as the two members of the Guard who paid a visit to John earlier that day had been. It could be part of the initial sweep, but Jacoby suspected that had been finished hours ago. It was unlikely these Guard members were there for anything routine.

Security had already discovered the one bread crumb he had no choice but to leave for them. The Guard knew it was likely he would pay Roth a visit, but they wouldn't know why. Not this soon. It should take at least a couple days before the Authority discovered what business he had with Roth he hoped. With any luck, it would be after he completed what he came to the surface to do.

Until then, they would assign a detail to watch the house, and a team would be ordered to monitor Roth's movements as well if they allowed him to leave at all. He escaped with the intent of killing Roth and his pregnant wife Serena, but he wouldn't hesitate to take out anyone who stood in his way of accomplishing his goal.

It looked like the team was leaving which didn't provide a clear answer for what stage of the investigation it was. It might still be a routine visit, or they could be headed to Roth's location to keep him safe if they had discovered anything about Phillipe's motive. He would have to make sure the team left and didn't position themselves to watch the house. Phillipe began contemplating his next move. It might be wise to enter the residence as soon as the team left.

The team turned back toward the door as someone else emerged. It was his old friend John Reed.

"Change of plans," Phillipe said to himself. "It looks like

I have another date with Christine."

Chapter Thirty-Three

Play Nice

Christine's face looked so pristine and innocent. Phillipe wondered if all humans were as trusting as her. If they were, they'd be foolish enough to befriend the pixies which would lead to their demise. It was to their benefit the human race wasn't aware of their existence.

'Why did we ever feel the need to hide from these creatures?'

Humans had the numbers on their side now. Even if all the cryptoids alive banned together, they would lose. Some of the magical ones would manage, of course, but they'd be persecuted as long as they lived. Their abilities being the only thing to keep them alive. The humans would figure it out. They were ignorant, but they weren't stupid. Some kind of trap capable of preventing magic from being used would be developed.

The Below originated long before the population of humans exploded. The belief was humans had the instinct to attack instead of learning to live together. Phillipe didn't disagree with that. *'Why were we the ones to run and live in secrecy? We had the numbers before population control was enforced. This world could've been ours.'*

He glanced back at Christine. The area under her left cheekbone was tight and shiny. It would discolor soon. She was still breathing, and he wondered how long he'd check to see if she still was. If anything was going to happen, it probably would've by now.

It took several minutes, but he found her phone. It was in her purse which was on the kitchen counter. A notepad was next to it, and he read the note she was working on when he knocked at the door.

'Hey!

Running out to meet John for lunch. I'll be home-'

Her parents would be back soon. There'd be less need to leave a note if she expected to be home before them. He looked at where she lay near the base of the stairs and considered moving her to John's apartment. *'Out of the question. People would notice someone carrying a lifeless body.'*

Phillipe picked her up and carried her to the front room, gently laying her on the couch. He moved her on her side, facing the back to keep her developing shiner a secret from anyone who may come home. He told himself he didn't feel bad for punching her when he filled a small towel with ice from the kitchen and placed it under her face where the swelling was worsening. It wasn't guilt. He did what he felt he had to do. It was because deep down, somewhere, he was a decent being. He was almost sure of it.

He grabbed her phone and sat on the couch near her feet. It was locked and needed a fingerprint to access it. Phillipe sighed and rolled his eyes. *'Too easy.'* He grabbed Christine's hand and tried one finger after another until it worked.

There were two texts from John. One explained he'd be late for their lunch because something came up, and the other promised to make it up to her. He scrolled up through their message history and found what he was looking for. A message she sent weeks ago telling John to come over when he could, followed by three hearts.

He typed out the exact reply. "Come over when you can," but left out the hearts. It was partly because he didn't know how to type them. *'Besides, any man canceling on a woman like her didn't deserve hearts.'* He looked at Christine and waited until the rise and fall of her chest told him she was still asleep.

'If she had only shut up.' Phillipe stared at the kitchen. His mouth watering over what he might find to eat. John was a bachelor, and his refrigerator reflected that. The best he'd eaten since coming to the top was the last time he paid Christine a visit.

It was worth her waking up while he was occupied. He rummaged through the contents while occasionally glancing back to see if she had moved. Phillipe pulled three containers out and opened them on the counter, eating directly from them. There was a pasta dish that wasn't too bad, some kind of meat smothered in a tangy sauce, and a bowl of cut fruit. He stuck his fork in a piece of meat and ate around it. John had explained how to use a microwave, but there were so many rules regarding what could be used in one and how long to heat food. Phillipe had barely payed attention. He regretted that now because whatever this was would probably be better heated up. It wasn't worth the risk of destroying anything in the Tucker's kitchen after he already knocked out their daughter.

'I didn't knock her out. I punched her, yes, but she knocked herself out when she tripped as she ran from me, falling into the banister.'

After he ate, he sat near her feet again and waited. He hoped John showed before her parents returned home, and he hoped Christine stirred before anyone walked through the door. He only meant to threaten her and wasn't planning on doing anything more than reminding John of what he could do if he chose.

'But she wouldn't let me get a word in!' As soon as she opened the door, she talked nonstop. She told him she was on her way out to meet John for lunch.

"Hi, Phillipe! I was just leaving."

"Hi." He wasn't sure if Christine heard because she kept talking.

"You're more than welcome to join us. I'm sure John won't mind. We're having sushi. You like sushi?"

"Sushi? John is busy right now. He sent me..."

"Of course you do. Everyone likes sushi. Just let me grab my purse, and we'll be on our way."

"Christine!" He'd been trying to speak since she opened the door, but couldn't.

It caught her attention, and she stared at him. Christine looked pissed like his tone assaulted her senses. Actually, she looked at him like he was the rude one, and that's what made him angry. That's when he hit her. The tactic worked the first time they met. It was worth a shot.

Phillipe didn't know how long it took, but he was about

to head back to the apartment, letting the chips fall where they may. Boredom was not his color. The phone dinged, and he saw John's text saying it wouldn't be long now. He decided to wait it out a little longer. Christine began to move and moan not long after the text. As soon as she started to come to, the front door opened, and the voices of a couple drifted into the house. *'Her parents.'*

He saw Christine's eyes had opened and leaned over to whisper, "Play nice," as sternly as he could manage while not speaking loud enough for her parents to hear him.

They walked into the front room as Christine sat up, gently cradling her now deeply bruised face. "Christine!" Her mom's voice was filled with concern, and she started for her daughter. When she noticed Phillipe, she stopped.

"What happened?" her father demanded, glaring at the stranger sitting in his house.

"That's Phillipe," Christine said. Her voice slurred the words like she had too much to drink. "He's fine. This was Natalie," she said, motioning to her face.

Chapter Thirty-Four

Denied

Lichten walked out of Masterson's office with his head hung low. His fate would be decided once Jacoby was captured. In all likelihood, his job was gone, but that decision wouldn't be left to Masterson alone. His judgment was certainly clouded given the events of the last few days. He knew well enough to involve the panel for this.

After a dismal showing in the appeal, Lichten had asked, "For centuries, you've been content. Never appealed. Never one wrong look over the decision handed down. What makes you so set on transitioning to the surface now?"

Phillipe slammed his fist onto Lichten's desk. "After thirteen hundred years, I believe I've waited long enough!" He had practically yelled in Lichten's face.

Because of the outburst, Lichten stamped the large red "DENIED" into Jacoby's file right then instead of waiting as was protocol. Judgements are never given in an appeal meeting for the purpose of protecting their employees. It's not uncommon for some to act rashly when receiving bad news. A letter gives them time to cool off before making it to the Authority building where Security would have already been put on alert in case they reacted poorly. It was a bad decision on Lichten's part. It was something he admitted in the report he wrote months ago.

Jacoby saw the stamp and leaned over Lichten's desk. His nostrils flared, and his cheeks reddened as he brought his face as close as he could manage to Lichten's. The fear tactic didn't work. Maybe it was his short stature, or the fact there hadn't been an issue with Jacoby's temper in well over a century. Either way, Lichten's reaction wasn't to be afraid, but was annoyed Jacoby honestly thought he could be a threat.

And, now he was. Jacoby was a threat to everything Lichten valued in life. His career, his good name, standing in the community, and ability to provide for his family were all at stake. If Masterson had a soft side, he'd have thought it almost poetic.

Detailing it in the appeal report wasn't enough. Actions that weren't necessarily illegal, but definitely out of character were to be reported by other means. Jacoby's outburst should've been investigated internally. It should've been Jacoby's job on the line, not Lichten's.

He was smart. Masterson wouldn't deny him that credit. "But he's lucky too." Masterson muttered to himself closing the files on his desk. There had been so many missed opportunities to stop him before he escaped, to curb the behaviors, to catch him doing something illicit. All of them slipped past his own staff.

There was a quote he read somewhere about complacency. It bred failure, and only the paranoid survived.

At the time, Masterson wanted to turn it into a poster and hang them on every wall of the Security offices, send some to the surface too.

"It wouldn't have mattered." Masterson walked across the office to close the door Lichten left open. "No one would've changed their ways."

He walked back to his desk and resumed the footage he'd been watching for hours. Jacoby made quick work at befriending Strickland. The tunnel used in the escape was on Strickland's post. Jacoby could've managed entering it without help, but he needed Security access. Without it, he wouldn't have got far. The doors in the tunnel will not open unless you're cleared to be there. Any attempt to disarm them, damage them, would trigger the alarm. Of course, that wasn't entirely true of the door to the windmill. It would open easily enough, but the alarm would sound. No one thought it possible for someone to make it to that point.

One corner of his lip snarled watching the two of them chat like old friends. Masterson would turn it off. He had everything he needed regarding how the escape was managed, but he hoped the footage would lead to the wolfsbane. If there was a crop of it in the Below, it would be destroyed.

The phone on his desk rang, and he paused the video. It was a welcome and needed distraction. "Masterson," he huffed into the receiver.

Liam Greene's voice crackled on the line. Masterson rolled his eyes. He was another one who dropped the ball in the investigation. If even just one of these who were entrusted with the safety and security of them all had done their job, it would've made the difference.

'But that's how I'm confident we'll catch him. It was more luck than brains working for him.'

"What do you got?" Masterson hoped it was Jacoby in chains, but he doubted the ability of anyone on the force at this point.

The line popped and hissed. It was never a smooth connection from the surface, but this was worse than usual.

"...appeared. We're...him now... Soon."

Masterson squinted his eyes in the hopes of hearing better. *'Appeared? Who? They have him now? Or not now, but soon.'* His mouth gaped and inhaled sharply. *'Jacoby!'*

"Trailing him..." Greene's voice kept cutting in and out.

"Jacoby?" Masterson tried to hide his excitement. "You have a lead?"

The line crackled, and Masterson worried they were disconnected. There had to be interference up top. Solar flares. Storms. The human government blamed anything they could think of when they tampered with the communication grid to throw people off about what was really happening.

"Should... custody tonight." Those were the only words of Greene's to come through.

"Jacoby?" Masterson practically yelled when he repeated his question.

"No."

He shook his head and threw his free hand up, shaking it. This was frustrating. He had to have misheard all the bits of the conversation he thought he grasped. *'If not Jacoby, who?'*

Greene answered like he could read Masterson's mind, and it was the one word of the entire phone call to come through crystal clear. As soon as the name was said, the call disconnected. "Mezzie."

Masterson cradled the handset and smiled. A peace settled over him for the first time since Jacoby escaped. It was a two for one. Mezzie had ditched Guard surveillance long before his time, but he was going to be the one responsible for bringing him to justice. He clasped his fingers behind his head and leaned back in his chair.

When the idea struck him, he almost dismissed it out of hand, but it could work. He looked down his legs and pictured them in pants. Humans didn't pay close attention. It was possible.

Somewhere in a box buried in a closet of his home was a pair of shoes. His late wife, bless her heart, had them specially made for him when he was promoted to Security Director. He made the attempt. They were surprisingly comfortable and walking in them wasn't as difficult as he'd guessed. They weren't him. He was proud of who he was and didn't need to pretend to be someone he wasn't. *'But this might be good enough cause for it.'*

He might be able to pull it off. A pair of pants to hide haunches, a pair of shoes designed to slip his hooves into while giving him the appearance of having feet, human feet. Masterson nodded as the look came together in his mind. He could slip up top and be present for the capture of not one, but both of the Below fugitives.

Chapter Thirty-Five

Authority Lineage

The sound which emitted from Simmons' throat could only best be described as a growl. John flinched and eyed the detective. For the very first time, it occurred to him he didn't know the cryptoid status of the Above personnel. In the Below, the lineage of the Security members wasn't made public knowledge, but word got around.

Some figure it out for themselves. When a Security member is regularly seen on patrol in uniform and then spied out with his family, it's easy to piece their origins together. The little girl clinging to the leg of the off duty officer might be a lycan in the same grade as your son. It stands to reason that man will always have a few days off around the time of the full moon. Once you reach the surface, that information is no longer readily available.

The Above Guard are never in uniform. They're meant to blend. Not only to fit in with humans, but their presence is supposed to be undetected by other cryptoids. There's nowhere to run in the Below, but it's a wide open world up top. They can't be expected to keep an eye on everyone, make sure they're staying in line, and intervene before anything goes south if everyone knows who they are.

For the first couple days when John was on his own after his acclimation and orientation, he had wondered. He'd examine the faces passing him on the street, standing in line, or near him in a crowd, and he'd wonder who among them worked for the Authority. It didn't take long at all for him to stop giving it a second thought.

John did what he came up here to do. He opened a bakery, and business boomed from the moment he opened the doors. He kept his head down and worked on doing what needed to be done. It didn't take long till he had made friends, and then came Christine.

He was used to living, really living. For someone who had grown up in the dark with his every movement monitored, having freedom and enjoying sunlight on his skin came natural to him. Not once in the five years he had lived Above had he ever wondered about the origins of the Guard.

Simmons' growl changed all that in a heartbeat. In his soul, he knew the detective was a werewolf. In that moment, it frightened him more than being sent to the Below for aiding Phillipe. There were drugs Simmons could take, plants, herbal treatments which would allow him to control when he transitioned. That meant he wasn't controlled by the full moon. Invisibility was a great defense, but it only protected you from sight. It did nothing to cover your scent, especially from a wolf.

The detective leaned forward with his arms on his legs, rubbing his hands together. "No," he said shortly. "We won't be leaving you here."

"It's what we had hoped to do," Boyd cut in quickly. "We wanted to have you stay as added surveillance and protection for Serena." He motioned to her midsection. "I don't have to explain to you how important this pregnancy is for others like us."

John nodded. A bred vampire was an extraordinary achievement. Their numbers were dwindling like everyone else's. Even one child could change that around. "But?"

"But Roth wouldn't have it," Simmons answered.

"Well," Serena's voice sounded flustered. "Can I get you anything? More tea?"

"No, thank you, ma'am," Boyd politely replied.

John shook his head without meeting her eyes.

Simmons' phone rang, and he jumped to his feet, welcoming the opportunity to remove himself from the conversation. "I have to take this." He excused himself before walking outside.

"Brendan is leery of us setting a trap," Boyd explained. "He thinks we're trying to lure Jacoby here, but that isn't true. The house is covered fully with surveillance. If he came anywhere near this house, we'd know."

"He's getting things in order right now, planning on leaving in the morning on an unexpected business trip. That's where you come in. We're going to have you tail him, stay by his side, unseen by all."

"I wanted to meet you," Serena said. "That's why you're here."

John looked at her, really looked at her. Before all he could notice was her beauty and the obvious signs of pregnancy. All he could see now was her fear. This was a woman who was about to give birth and should be at the height of a very exciting time of her life. It was overshadowed by Phillipe and whatever his agenda was with her and Brendan.

In her eyes, he could see she was scared for herself and her husband. Mostly, she was terrified about anything befalling her unborn child.

"Why is he after you?" John asked.

She glanced at Boyd as if asking for permission.

Boyd looked at the floor, but waved a hand toward her as if to say it's up to you.

"He's after my husband. He wants revenge."

"For what?"

"Roth murdered Jacoby's parents." Simmons spoke from the doorway where no one had noticed him return, causing all three of them to jump.

"Phillipe's parents?" John was shocked. He had no idea it was something so sinister. "Roth killed them?"

"It's not that simple," Boyd said. "He had to keep his cover. Either he participated in their death, or he was found out himself."

"Easy decision if you ask me." Simmons walked in the room and stood near his partner's chair. "When it comes down to it, every single one of us would choose saving our own skin over needlessly dying next to someone already in receipt of a death sentence."

A shiver went down John's spine, and he wondered, not for the first time that day, if Simmons was making a sideways crack toward him because the detective already knew of his involvement with Phillipe. "But why wait this long? Does it have anything to do with the pregnancy?"

Simmons laughed and patted his partner on the shoulder, nodding to the door. "Nah. This is all because thirteen hundred years ago some idiot in the Below thought it was a good idea to tell a sad little boy his dad died in a drowning accident, and his mother had died in childbirth. I guess they never expected him to uncover the truth."

He turned to Serena, and said, "Ma'am, as always, it's a pleasure. I have to get back to the office. I think I speak for all of us when I say respectfully, I hope we never have to meet again."

Chapter Thirty-Six

Whirly-Do's

Mezzie materialized in a smoke filled darkened hallway. The two men nearby hadn't noticed, or hadn't cared, about his sudden appearance. Their interest was in drugs, or worse. The music from the live band was loud even in the far corners of the club. His head already pounded from the distance he teleported. The farther he traveled the more sickened he felt when he arrived.

"Hey!" One of the men finally paid attention to him.

He lifted his head in a swift nod to acknowledge the transient waste of space in the hall.

"Got a light?" The guy lifted a cigarette to his lips.

He reached into his pocket and summoned a lighter. When he pulled it out, he tossed it at the wretch. "Keep it," he said, walking past the guy and his friend.

When he reached the end of the hallway, he put his hand on his head and grabbed a pair of sunglasses out of thin air to pull down over his eyes. The music was enough to make his head throb without adding colored lenses to cover the bright yellow of his irises. The glasses would do until he recovered.

It was ten till nine. The watch on his arm changed style three times until he decided on one more fitting for the area and not too flashy. It shouldn't take more than ten minutes. His chem trail would've been picked up by the Guard as soon as he showed himself in Rotterdam.

He skirted the edges of the crowded dance floor as he made his way to the bar and ordered three drinks. The shot was to get the party started. He also ordered his favorite stout beer and the froo, froo, froofiest mixed drink he knew. It was heavenly to be in a country where he could drink what he wanted without worry about what was going into the glass, or if the glass was even clean.

There wasn't an open table, but he found a spot along a wall to stand relatively undetected. He could keep an eye on the door and watch as people came inside. The Guard were hard to spot from a distance, but not impossible. They'd send at least four teams. Two would stay outside to monitor the entrances while the other two would pose as club goers to find him. Therein lay the tricky part. He needed to be seen, to be found out, but they couldn't get close enough to put a tracking device on him.

Things had changed a lot over the years. The golden days of scanning your clothes or flesh for where they attached one to remove it were long gone. The Guard could put something in food or drink to keep tabs on anyone. It was short term, but it was effective while it lasted. Mezzie had even heard tale of a spray that if inhaled would stay in the nasal cavity for weeks. He wanted them to see him and to follow him, hoping he'd lead them to Phillipe. The last thing he needed was for them to have the upper hand in attempting to capture him.

'*Heads up,*' he thought, putting his empty glass on the tray of a waitress as she walked by. These two look like prime suspects. Their clothes fit the atmosphere, but their hair and demeanor did not. They looked like they raided a college student's closet to try to blend. Sometimes you shouldn't leave the house wearing it even if the shoe does fit.

They went to the far side of the club, so he focused on their every detail, committing it to memory, from their looks to the sound of their voice to their smell. If they came within twenty feet of him, he'd sense their presence. It was one of the many perks of being a djinn.

The Guard would follow protocol and stagger the entrances. A few groups came through the door before the next couple he was looking for arrived. It was a pair of ladies this time. They fit the profile of clubbers perfectly, but the stench of the Authority dripped off them. He concentrated and added them to his memory right alongside the other two.

He watched as they worked their way through the dance floor. His partying days preceded him, but it wasn't a bad idea to check there first. They had their little whirly-do's and zip-a-doodle's out, testing the air of everyone they neared for any sign of allohuman qualities amongst the patrons. They reached the other side of the dance floor and moved slowly along the opposite side of the club that the first team had done.

In a few minutes, he'd have to make his move. He chugged his beer regretting not ordering another from the waitress when he had a chance. The night was young. He could slip into any joint in the city he chose once he lost his tail.

Before they got too close, he stepped out from the wall, intentionally bumping into somebody. His sunglasses fell to the floor with a little help and a nod from him. The people nearby stopped to see what was going on, primarily if there'd be a fight. Mezzie ruled that out with a blink in the direction of the man he collided with, and the guy moved on like nothing happened. He picked his sunglasses off the floor, but before putting them on, he made sure to cast the slightest glance in the direction of the female Guard team.

One of them caught the flash of yellow from his eyes. She motioned to her partner and spoke into the pendant of her necklace.

Mezzie shook his head. Technology was expanding too quickly. It wouldn't be long until he was outdated and his abilities obsolete. Acting alarmed, he made his way to the exit, forcing down a smile the whole way. The teams outside would be watching for him with the description from the woman with the necklace before he felt the fresh night air.

Once outside, he inhaled deeply. One team was close, but not near the line trying to gain entrance. He could make a run for it without them tagging him. There was an alley across the street, and he darted down it after making sure he was being followed, transporting to a different part of the city about halfway through. When he reappeared behind a building in the business district on Franklin Avenue, he hurried to one of his many safe havens. He'd be off the radar before the Guard made it anywhere close.

Chapter Thirty-Seven

Finding Emilia

Phillipe wandered through the empty hallway disconnecting the rejects from the rest of the school. Donnelly sent him to the office to seek out bandages as soon as the blood began to pour from his hand. Shouts of how he needed to bring back supplies to clean up the classroom followed as the door closed behind him. It was *his* mess, not the janitor's is what his teacher had pointed out. *'How compassionate.'*

When he reached the end where the hall connected to the main part of the school, he turned in the opposite direction of where he needed to go. His hand was bleeding heavily, and the front of his shirt was drenched in his own blood. If the secretary called the orphanage to send him home for the day, the pain he was experiencing could be in vain.

It was the ultimate goal, of course. Partly. He needed to find Emilia, to see if she was alright. Images of her father's anger and what he may have done to her had been flashing through his mind ever since he didn't see her arrive that morning. Before he left school in a rage to confront him, he needed to double check, to see if she ever made it to class.

He carefully walked down the main hallway. It had been so long since his one day, not even a full day, of regular class. He passed three doors thinking each was the classroom where he once sat so eagerly full of hope over the idea of making friends. The memory had faded. That coupled with how hard the school tried to keep the unwanted away from the mainstream students, not allowing them in this part of the school unless absolutely necessary, made it difficult for him to know which room it was.

It saddened him. That classroom was his only connection to normalcy. Nothing about him or his life was typical. Phillipe's heart beat faster and sweat collected along his brow. He couldn't be sure if it was from his injury or his thoughts.

A door opened, and he quickly turned in the opposite direction he had been headed. The excuses were firing away for whatever was about to be said. They would all be truthful to an extent. He did need to find the office.

When no one confronted him, he glanced back in time to see a faun turn the corner at the end of the hall. *'No,'* he thought. *'She went into a different class.'*

Not sure if the young girl was on an errand or returning from one, he needed to be quick. He picked up the pace, headed to Emilia's classroom to peek inside to see if she was there. As soon as he reached the door, it swung open, as did the others in the hallway one by one. They were being released for lunch.

He waited, amid the sneers and snarky remarks as

everyone filed out around him. Then she was there, no more than two feet away. Relief flooded over him, but it was short lived.

Emilia looked directly at him. He grinned and waved, keeping his injured hand out of sight as much as he could. She'd worry if she saw it, and he didn't want that. There's no way she could miss him, but she turned and slid down the hall away from him.

'*What was that?*' he wondered. His first reaction was confusion and hurt over being shunned. '*No, she's not used to seeing me in the halls of the main school. That's how she missed me.*'

"Emilia," he said, heading after her. He darted around the other students who were still filing into the halls from their classes. "Emilia!" He had to raise his voice to be heard, but he didn't want to yell. None of the staff took kindly to the rejects tucked away out of sight and mind. They'd see him as a disturbance and report him.

No response. She didn't even slow down. He ran in front of her and blocked her path. "Hey!" His breathing was shallow, but it was from fear of getting caught. "I didn't see you this morning. I was worried."

"I had to be here early," she said. Emilia glanced nervously at her friend then continued to move past him.

Phillipe's face reddened. He didn't understand why she was acting so different around these other kids. She had never treated him this way. Then again, the only time he'd been around her in a group was outside before the bell rang, and they had a minute or two tops before they had to go inside.

"Emilia!" He yelled at her standing right where she left him with his fists clenched at his sides. The blood pouring out of his palm ran down his fingers and dripped on the floor.

She flinched and paused for a moment then kept walking.

He stormed up behind her, and yelled again, "What's your problem?"

Emilia glanced anxiously at her friend who threw her hands up, and said, "This is all you Em. I've got a class."

Phillipe stood as tall as he could in front of his girlfriend, but didn't reach where her elongated scales met her human torso. He stared up at her and watched as she glanced around at the other kids walking by, and it seemed like she was casting pleading eyes at them hoping they'd help her out in some way. "Well?" he asked.

She took a deep breath before finally looking at him. "Phillipe, I'm sorry. I was going to find a way to talk to you later. I swear. It's just that... Your hand?" She gasped. "Are you bleeding?'

He scoffed considering how long he'd been right there without her noticing before glancing at his hand. It was covered in red. *'Good thing vampires are almost extinct. This might have been a bigger problem.'* His eyes twinkled, and he chuckled. There were other creatures who desired blood just maybe not as much. Some of them had to be in the nearby classrooms, crawling out of their skin from the scent, acting like addicts wanting a fix or rabid dogs.

"Phillipe?"

"It was the only way I could make sure you're alright," he

said softly.

"Me? You did this?"

"To get out of class. You weren't at the fence this morning."

Emilia softened and took his good hand. She led him a few feet down the hall and pulled him into an empty classroom right as the bell rang. "I have to go. I'm sorry. I'm going to get into trouble."

Phillipe nodded and smiled, caressing her hand with his. "I understand. I only wanted to see if you were okay."

She snatched her hand back from him. "I'm fine. It's just…"

"Your dad." Phillipe looked at the floor. It was easy to guess what was coming. He'd heard it before.

"Yeah," she said with tears in her voice. "I'm sorry, Phillipe. It's over."

Chapter Thirty-Eight

Franklin Avenue

It was a bit overcast the day he stepped outside which wasn't quite the clouds parting, allowing the beams of the sun to cascade around him lifting him in a heavenly glow look he was hoping for, but it did help his adjustment to the light. The dreary mood the sky set would break when the fugitives were caught allowing the rays to warm his shoulders then.

A team was waiting for him in the windmill and led him to the car over a mile away. He passed on the ATV they had ready to take him to it. These fools might be accustomed to such worrisome and dangerous looking craft, but he was not. Besides, his feet would be exposed. If anything happened to his shoes, he'd be out of luck. They were his only pair, and he'd be willing to bet faun shoes weren't readily available up top.

Mezzie had been spotted several times since his arrival in Rotterdam. The Guard had been chasing him for centuries. The hunt was easier with the ability to detect the residue left behind after he shifted.

'Shifted.' Masterson chuckled softly. *I'd be showing my age if I said that out loud.'*

The team talked incessantly on the drive to the main office, primarily Detective Olsen. He barely listened. Intel had been drifting down to the Below for days. Every detail, every movement, even every instance where nothing was uncovered had been committed to memory. He already had the one key to unlocking this case the Guard hadn't yet found. He knew where Mezzie and Jacoby were.

Detective Adam Morris met them at the top of the stairs when they arrived. His spiel bounced off Masterson's ears as they entered the office, heading straight to the conference room where operations for the case had been set up. He caught enough of it to get the gist of what Morris was trying to update him.

"Simmons and Boyd are in the field working with a confidential informant. I've called them back to the office for a report."

'A confidential informant?' Masterson resisted an eye roll. He knew their secret weapon was an invisible man.

"I have a team running point on the djinn, but they're tracking a new chem trail."

When Masterson didn't reply, he continued. "It's since you arrived, sir."

Masterson looked around the room and tried not to smile. They had everything displayed, every piece of evidence. There were pictures of suspects hung up. Some already crossed out. The Guard was being thorough. He'd give them that, but they lacked experience. They didn't have the gut instincts for real detective work, and it showed.

A long table in the center of the room was covered in files, notebooks and various other tidbits still being rifled through. Masterson swept his arm over a large section of it, knocking everything to the floor. The room which had been filled with a constant buzz of background chatter from everyone talking at once as they continued working with each other on the case instantly fell silent.

He set his bag on one of the chairs, and the zipper was the only noise to be heard when he opened it. That and a fly buzzing somewhere nearby, possibly in one of the other offices. Fauns were cursed with ears of gold.

From the bag, he pulled out a map of Rotterdam and unrolled it on the table. He'd been studying it since Mezzie first appeared at a dance club two nights ago. "Where's the newest location?"

One of the aides began stuttering and flipping through his notebook. "It's... It's uh... The corner of High Street and-"

"Mark it on the map," Masterson barked.

The chatter picked up again slowly, but this time there was a sense of apprehension to it. His reputation preceded him, as it should. No one wanted to be the one to cross him.

Morris picked up where he left off droning on about where his detectives were positioned and who was working what angle. It was not only boring and a waste of time, but a waste of resources too. They were spreading themselves too thin which is exactly what Mezzie wanted.

He looked around the room while the aide found the newest location on the map. "Coffee?" He boldly interrupted Morris' update.

"Coffee?" Detective Morris blinked in disbelief. He

hadn't expected such a nonchalant attitude from the head of the Authority. "Get him a coffee," he ordered the nearest person to him.

The aide looked up when he finished and saw Masterson watching him. A small cry flew from his lips before he could catch it, and he stumbled trying to move away from the table as quickly as he could.

Masterson studied the new marking and smiled. "Franklin Avenue, boys. That's where he's at."

Morris didn't say a word. He took a step forward trying to see what Masterson saw on the map that he hadn't.

"Did you hear me?" Masterson's voice grew loud. "Pull everyone to Franklin Avenue."

When the reaction time wasn't immediate, he yelled, "Now!"

The room erupted as everyone set to work on it. He heard Morris repeat the order to Simmons and Boyd about coming to the office before returning to Franklin Avenue. An aide walked over with his coffee in one hand. The other hand held a pile of napkins under the mug. The aide's hands shook so violently it was a wonder there was anything left to drink.

Masterson took the cup and sat down. He blew into it before taking a sip, watching the commotion and chaos he'd caused. He didn't work his literal tail off to get to where he was not to have people jump to action when he spoke. The day was young, and he hoped to have both the fugitives in custody by dinner time. His wife wasn't expecting him home for a week. It'd give him time to enjoy how the other half lived while interrogations began.

"Sir."

He took another sip. The water quality was better on the surface, and this was easily the best coffee he'd ever drank. It'd be hard to go back to the swill they brewed at home. He finally looked up at Morris.

"Are you going to clue me in as to why I just sent all my teams to an area we've already cleared?"

Masterson smirked at the young pup. The detective was a child compared to the years he had on him. His young age showed by assuming it was his place to question the head boss. He's also the reason things got as out of hand as they had. If he'd taken the initial alarm seriously, Jacoby would've been picked up before he made it to the city. *Ah, but then you wouldn't have Mezzie within your grasp.*

"Yes." Masterson sat up straight and lifted his cup to the aide who delivered it requesting a refill. "Just as soon as you explain how this investigation has been fumbled in such an extraordinarily comical manner."

Chapter Thirty-Nine

Is Everything Alright?

John made it back to his apartment long after he and Christine had plans for lunch. Ever since Phillipe showed up, he'd let her down time and again. He was always running late or rescheduling, and let's not forget the threat of a fist to the face. How she managed to forgive that and see past Phillipe's faults was beyond him. It made him love her even more for being the kind of person with such strength of character, but also made him realize he didn't deserve her. This was his fault. Phillipe was invading their lives because he didn't do what needed to be done as soon as the emergency message appeared on his phone. Every second that had passed since only made coming clean more difficult.

To his surprise, his phone wasn't littered with notifications wondering where he was and why he wasn't answering. There was only one from her telling him to come over when he can, but it was sent quite a while ago. He hoped it meant she had been tied up in something and was running behind schedule herself, but he had doubts he'd be that lucky. Either she had her own emergency to deal with, one where he once again wasn't around to offer to help her, or she was done with him and tired of being disappointed. Neither had a better outcome for him and their relationship.

He checked his appearance in the bathroom. As soon as the door closed on the tiny room, he noticed a florally scent. He closed his eyes and inhaled through his nose trying to figure out the source. An image of Serena passed through his mind. It was her. This was how she smelled when they met. John didn't think he'd come that close to her, but he obviously did. He couldn't see Christine when he smelled like another woman.

John took a deep breath and sighed. Whether he had time or not, he was going to have to shower before leaving. He sent a quick text saying he was sorry, and he'd be ready in twenty minutes.

He wrapped himself in a towel when he was through, running through the apartment as he dressed trying not to forget anything. Phillipe still hadn't returned which meant he'd be able to leave easily without someone causing a reason for delay like was typical of him. It wasn't the least bit reassuring. If he wasn't hidden away here, he was out in the world at risk of being caught and bringing John down with him.

There was still no word from Christine. He prayed she was livid and giving him the silent treatment. He'd hate to think of what could've happened that would prevent her from being able to get ahold of him. He tried to keep a clear mind, but those thoughts, waking nightmares, found their way in anyway. As soon as he'd vanquish one, six more would be standing ready to take its place.

"I'm on my way," he sent, standing at the door to his apartment. He locked it behind him. It might deter thieves, but Phillipe had his own ways to let himself inside. Briefly, he wondered if he wasn't actually working with Mezzie. It would explain so much of what Phillipe was capable of doing.

'No,' John told himself. *Forget all of that for now. Christine is all that matters.'*

He ran down the stairs and out the building door planning on walking the normal route to her parents' house. He'd stick to the sidewalks along the street instead of taking a shortcut through yards and alleys. If she was on her way to him, on foot or driving, she'd pass him. Really he wanted to take it slow to avoid showing up out of breath like he was in a panic even if he was teetering on one.

As soon as his eyes adjusted to the blinding sun, he sensed something was wrong. At first, he believed it was from his worried thoughts about Christine. He wouldn't be able to breathe easy until he heard from her or made it to her parents' house to see her in person. It didn't take a full block for him to question if that was really it, or if it was the only thing causing him to feel that way.

It wasn't until he was about to turn the corner when it hit him. There was supposed to be a car there. Obviously, he wasn't supposed to know where the Guard was placed keeping a lookout for Phillipe, but he had made a few of them. A silver sedan had been parked just around this corner since a few hours after Phillipe showed up in his bakery. The two Guard members sitting in the front seat varied depending on the day, but the car was always there.

John looked back at his apartment building and scanned the cars on the street on either side of the block. The surveillance was gone. There had been a car watching his building. He wasn't able to prove it, but a similar car with two people in the front seat had been parked on the street for as long as the other one had been on the corner. The disappearance of one car might not measure too high on his radar. They could be investigating a lead, or he could've been wrong in his belief they were associated with the Guard at all. But both cars? No, something had happened. He began walking again ticking off everything in his mind.

'Phillipe was gone.'

'Simmons received a call bringing him and Boyd back to the office.'

'The cars he was certain were assigned to watch for Phillipe had also disappeared.'

'There's been nothing from Christine this whole time when we had plans today.'

Christine wasn't a part of it. Not hearing from her was a coincidence. Maybe Phillipe finally messed up and was caught, or about to be apprehended. If that was the case, he felt fairly confident Simmons would make him aware even if he couldn't provide too many details.

'Or was it? Phillipe went to her once already.'

He picked up his pace wanting to get there as quickly as possible. It was a mental struggle to stay on the sidewalk. He walked the rest of the block trying to convince himself everything was okay. He was only being paranoid. Another call went to voice mail, and he panicked. At the corner, he cut across into an alley and sprinted the rest of the way there taking as many shortcuts as he could.

When he got to her door, he didn't bother waiting to compose himself. Winded and gasping for breath, he rang the bell then pounded the knocker repeatedly. Her father answered the door. "John!" He sounded quite happy to see him, but it was brief.

"Is everything alright?" He asked when John didn't have enough air to answer.

John nodded and held his hand up, waving as if to say he's fine.

"Did you run here? Whatever for?" Her father was eyeing him suspiciously now. "Well, come in then. It seems to be the day for oddities around here. You'll fit right in."

Chapter Forty

End of the Road

From a table near the windows of the little café, Mezzie watched the commotion outside. It wouldn't be much of a fuss to the average person, but he knew what he was seeing and what was truly happening. A Guard team was being put in place.

He slapped some bills on the table and headed out the door for a closer look. The car was parked down the street from the apartment building he materialized in last night. One of the tenants saw the smoke from his entrance and called for help. It was an amusing sight, and he watched it all unfold across the street blending right in with the rest of the gawkers who had gathered.

The Guard had already investigated it and left, presumably after determining he was no longer in the area. It wasn't their first error since he arrived in Rotterdam. Now, he had to wonder why they were back.

Most likely, they were hoping to find something they missed, some small clue which would lead them straight to the djinn. Everyone wanted to be the one to capture him. A bust like that would be legend making.

Mezzie kept to the far side of the street from the building as he walked. Their gadgets and gizmos were in hand, and he was probably in close enough range to trigger a reading. It was no cause for worry because the remaining chem trail inside the building from his arrival would be stronger.

He didn't stop this time to watch them work. An idea was forming, and he hoped he was wrong. There was only one way to find out. He ran through a list of places he popped in and out of since arriving, and whittled the list down to a handful located not far from this one.

One at a time, he walked by each of the locations, or close enough to get a good look. Each of them had a team watching it. *'That's an interesting new development.'*

Franklin Avenue was a good twenty minutes away if he hustled, and he despised walking anywhere. It was time consuming and unnecessary when he could arrive at any destination with a simple thought. Today, he'd have to rely on his feet.

'It's bad news for Phillipe,' he thought. An unassuming car drove by with a young man and woman in the front seat. *'The Guard,'* he scoffed.

Mezzie could smell them. He didn't care who argued the logic behind his belief, but he was sure he could sniff them out of any guise anywhere. The teams always had the same look to them, dressed up, casual, business attire, and so on. They always matched. *'Look around!'* He scanned the people on the street looking for anyone who might be together. *'Dress and jeans. Office wear and band t-shirts.'* If they wanted to blend, they'd change up their outfits, so they weren't always matching.

That wasn't all. They had the same arrogance lingering around them like a fog. It was a combination of having pride in their work, feeling good about themselves because they believed in what they did, and a little cockiness, maybe even a feeling of superiority for being right in front of the humans without them having a clue. They reeked of it, and anyone could catch a whiff of it if they recognized the odor.

One of two things had happened. Phillipe had been apprehended, and they hoped to bring in the djinn too. Mezzie considered it briefly. *'No, he's still on the run.'* If he had been caught, it'd be big news. *'Or would it?'* He stopped on the sidewalk and people behind him muttered angrily as they sidestepped past. *'How many know the search is ongoing? Or do they think he's been caught?'* The Guard wouldn't want their operations to be widely spread information.

If Phillipe is still free, then they're trying to set a trap for him. *'Good luck,'* he scoffed. It was both good news and bad news for the little guy. On the one hand, Mezzie's plan had worked. The Guard believed he was helping Phillipe and had probably even orchestrated the escape. He'd provided a little distraction and hoped it was enough for Phillipe to do what he needed because this was the end of the road for him.

There was too much focus placed on him. The Guard were monitoring these places in the hopes he'd return to them or nearby, but he made sure lightning never struck the same place twice. It wasn't safe for him in Rotterdam. *'It was never safe here for someone like me, but I've outgrown my welcome.'*

He wished he'd had a chance to talk to Phillipe, but wherever he was, whoever was helping him, he was staying off the map. No one Mezzie had contacted had any information. Planning and successfully executing an escape from the Below was impressive enough, but he had managed to make arrangements for the surface too. *'Maybe he's actually a djinn.'* Mezzie smiled at his own joke.

It really was a shame. Rotterdam was a great city. It had plenty to offer without considering the company one might have. It was one of many cities across the world used by the Authority to place their kind when they surfaced.

As he walked he considered the downsides to his freedom. He was always on the run. The Authority kept pretty busy having two worlds to reign over, but he would always be on their list. For the moment, Phillipe was public enemy number one, but it wouldn't last. He would be captured. Mezzie was certain of it. For some reason, he hung around in Rotterdam which meant he had business here. It would be his downfall. If he had left the city as soon as he arrived, there'd be a chance for him. A rather large chance considering he didn't give off a presence of natural mysticism which could be tracked. If he was wrong and Phillipe managed to stay free, he'd still drop down on the pecking list. Their focus would always be on Mezzie. It wasn't anything he'd ever done, but it was what he was capable of doing which scared them.

It's why he could never get comfortable, could never settle anywhere. Friendships had to remain at arm's length and were fleeting. Relationships were out of the question. He fumbled with the tsavorite stone in his pocket. *'At least until I find Thalia.'*

Home was never home for long. He had to stay moving. It was a matter of time until they found him. He'd slip up eventually, get too cocky in his belief he was better than them, smarter and let his defenses fall. When the day came, he'd show them and the world a reason to fear him. If they took him down, the entire Below would be exposed in the process.

He turned the corner onto Franklin Avenue and headed to the Mystic Apothecary owned by an old friend. Mezzie snickered quietly. Old was right. Before pushing the door open and becoming assaulted by the overwhelming blend of herb and floral scents from the rows of creams and lotions displayed on antique furniture also for sale, he paused to inhale the aroma from the bakery down the street. It was heavenly, and he vowed to pay it a visit before leaving town.

'And it's time for Ames and I to have a serious discussion,' he thought, walking inside. Ames was helping a customer looking for a cream to decrease her appetite. Mezzie had to turn away to avoid the woman seeing his grin and jumping to the conclusion he was mocking her. It amused him people actually believed the right mix of herbs would work these wonders when only magic could pull off these tricks. *'There are questions he's been avoiding for far too long. Perhaps we'll chat over one of those chocolate croissants I've been smelling since I arrived.'*

Chapter Forty-One

Four Days

Phillipe almost regretted uncovering the truth. Dying in childbirth was a far better alternative, and he was thankful he'd been fed the lie as a child. At some point as an adult he deserved to learn what really caused his parents' deaths. It was safe to assume if no one had come forward in the first thirteen centuries of his life, they weren't ever going to tell him what really happened the night he was born.

The appearance of Kayda in the canal would've stunned anyone. Even a cryptoid could be taken aback to see a water dragon make her presence known. The only window of opportunity his mother had ended a few moments after she disappeared beneath the surface with Phillipe tucked into her wing. Those few moments after giving birth while listening to the fate of her husband when she was exhausted and her body weak from labor were all she had. There was never a chance for her to survive.

Once the sailors caught wind of her presence, they rushed to her thinking she had been attacked. They offered her aide, but it was short lived. When the truth of her situation was discovered, she became a prisoner.

Four days. That's how long she lived after the night her world ended. Esther Jacoby spent four days in a cellar jail cell heavily chained because of her association with the nonhuman beasts her captors feared. Whether they thought someone may save her or she had powers herself, they did their all to ensure she remained in custody.

Four days without medical treatment. A midwife was never called to tend to her. His mother grew weaker with every passing hour as she bled from a poor birth experience, mostly caused unintentionally by Kayda. The beast who saved him didn't realize the damage she caused to his mother.

For four days, she barely ate or drink. They were too afraid of what his mother may be capable of if she had her strength. Besides, the beasts they feared could survive on less being nonhuman after all. Four long days passed with crowds chanting outside.

For four long unending days, she suffered. Esther starved and begged for water. She bled, and her body was ravaged by infection. Her temperature increased as her color drained. On the fourth day, well into the night, she finally succumbed, having no reason to fight for her own survival, nothing to live for any longer.

It weighed on him. His mother's only crimes were falling in love with his father and bringing him into the world. The only people who ever truly loved him were gone, and it was his fault. His life, his whole existence was the reason they were discovered. If not for him, they'd have been able to escape to a safer place where their lives would've continued on as they should have done.

No one cared at all about their fates except for him. The Authority granted Roth a pass for the role he played in their deaths. It was just another day in life Above for them. Yet, he went to his office day after day for centuries preparing cryptoids to ascend. He drilled into them the protection the Above Guard offered. He assured them nothing would befall them because the Guard would swoop in like saviors on a white horse before anything got too far if they were discovered.

'It was all a lie.'

Everything about his life wasn't the truth. The building blocks for their governing system were nothing more than a propaganda campaign steering their own kind away from unveiling what was really happening. The Authority didn't care about any of them. They were weeding out the population of the Below for their own survival, but once they hit the surface, it was all a façade. The Guard was obviously a part of the charade.

Phillipe paced the front room of his home. He walked back and forth dozens of times before he realized he had even stood up. Once he noticed what he was doing, he expanded the track he was making to include the hallway and the kitchen. With every pass, he glanced at the counter which was missing a sink. It infuriated him even more.

They murdered his father. They allowed his mother to wither away until her own hopelessness took her life. They trapped him in this prison, never allowing him to feel the sun warm his skin, and for what?

'To protect a vampire.'

Somehow the life of one blood drinking immortal weighed more than his entire family and their lineage. Vampire numbers were dwindling, but his people were almost extinct. He was the end of his kind. For reasons he didn't understand, reasons he was sure would never be explained if he questioned it, the Authority was willing to let his kind die out to save Roth.

And, sadly, he was still alive. People talk. It's an unwritten truth that's not limited to the surface dwellers. There's plenty enough gossip to go around the Below that drips down the sewers from time to time.

'That's what I'll do then,' he thought, gathering the files off the table.

"If it's going to end with me, I'm going out fighting." He went to his room and wrote out a list of all the known exits from the Below. There were far more he was sure than the ones he could remember.

It would be difficult, but not impossible. As one of the oldest creatures in their world, everyone knew him. He was a loner, yes, but not untrustworthy. It would be easy for him to gain access to what and who he needed to accomplish this. Time was the one thing on his side. If it took another century, both he and Roth would likely still be around for him to accomplish it.

The first thing he had to do was plan his escape. He'd watch the Security team, learn their schedules and their weaknesses. Then, he'd have to locate Roth. He could search for Roth's identification number easily, but he couldn't search for his file without cause. All personal files were extremely confidential and accessing them without permission was heavily monitored. When he was ready, he'd risk the search to find Roth's location.

They wouldn't capture him. He'd see to that. If they took him down, it'd be the last thing he ever did. Dying during an escape attempt only meant he wouldn't have to live with the regret and have the would've, should've, could've running through his mind for the rest of his life. Once he made it to the surface, he already knew what he had to do.

Chapter Forty-Two

Hiding in Wait

Everything about Brendan Roth repulsed him. It didn't help he'd spent years planning how to exact his revenge of his parents' deaths out on this one man, this vampire, but Phillipe tried to convince himself he wouldn't have cared for Roth much if he met him under different circumstances.

For one thing, he was a *vampire*. It was a classification of one of the lowest of the cryptoids stalking the streets of the free world. They had never been deemed safe to live on the surface. By safe, it didn't mean low risk for the humans wandering around their pathetic lives with blinders on, having no clue what was actually going on around them. It meant the likelihood of the Below being exposed was minimal. Humans were an acceptable collateral damage. Give any human a list of cryptoids and ask them to pick which they believe could most likely be real, and they'll pick vampires almost every single time. Vampires, bigfoot and unicorns always top their belief list. Sadly, those terrified wasps of the mammalian order all but caused the extinction of the last two. The only ones of those cryptoids still alive and well have to exist beneath the surface.

That's why the vampires weren't sent up here. If they were discovered, most humans wouldn't be surprised. They would accept the scary campfire stories as truth. None of them would wonder where they came from, where they'd been hiding for so long. The Below would be protected, in more ways than one.

Not only would the secret of its existence remain safe, but none of the dwellers beneath the surface had to deal with these irritating creatures. When they stepped out of line, they were taken in by the Guard and sent Below, but no one ever saw them again.

Phillipe watched him from the house across the street. He had been keeping close tabs for a couple days until the Guard intervened. Roth had barely been outside since. He'd seen enough to turn his stomach. This creature passed as a man living his a normal life and partaking in everything regular humans took for granted.

He'd leave for work with his wife walking him to the car, kissing her goodbye. When he returned, he walked inside with a smile on his face like life was good. He acted as though he couldn't easily kill at will and had before, probably numerous times more than Jacoby was aware, and was not any different from the others on his street.

He'd ventured closer once on his first night in Rotterdam, before the Guard had correctly determined why he had come. Under the cover of darkness, he stole upon their lawn and watched them through their windows. Humans had their words for it, but he had his own. It wasn't stalking; it was studying the enemy. He wasn't a peeping

Tom; he was collecting Intel.

It only fueled his anger to see them so happy. They laughed over their dinner and held hands while watching a movie. Roth didn't have the right! He shouldn't be allowed to continue, to enjoy life, to have a life at all even if it was a miserable existence which it clearly wasn't, not after what he did, not after he stole Phillipe's life from him.

Phillipe watched as Roth placed his hand on his wife's protruding belly. The movements of their unborn child spread a grin on his face. His eyes twinkled as he looked lovingly at Serena.

There had been a plan. He always intended to murder Roth while his wife watched just as his mother had to endure. Then it'd be her turn. The only question was whether he'd let the child live. As an orphan, the baby would be sent Below, but there were others of its kind there to take it in and raise it, unlike how it had been for him.

Watching the two of them together, he began to reconsider. It might be more pleasing to allow Roth to watch as everything he held dear was stripped from him before he took his life as well. Both scenarios played out beautifully in his mind. He'd play it by ear when the time came to strike.

Then the Guard interfered and prevented him from getting too close. Since then, he's been watching from the now abandoned house across the street.

'Abandoned,' he laughed to himself. The owners were certainly disposed to say the least.

He hadn't been back to the apartment since he discovered John was working with the Guard. In fact, he hadn't left the house since that day. His so called friend swore he hadn't given up any information about him, and he supposed that was true. If he had, the Guard would've swarmed John's apartment building while he slept to capture him.

Still, he didn't like how John played them both. He pretended to give Phillipe a safe place to hide while also acting as if he was helping the Guard. If he really had no intention of giving away his location, he should've said something. John could've easily let him know what was going on and what he was doing about it, but he chose to stay quiet.

In a perfect world, John would have his day once Phillipe finished what he came to the surface to do, and that day may still come to pass. The world was far from perfect. That much was indisputable. John may very well live out his days with this period of his life remaining nothing more than a sore memory. Time would tell.

For now, it looked like Phillipe would have to act fast. They were preparing to move Roth and maybe his wife. If John squealed after their fall out the last time he visited Christine, they'd be wise to move Serena too. A few items had already been brought out of the house and carried away in vehicles driven by the Guard.

Phillipe had watched every movement carefully. He checked for people talking when it appeared no one was around. Extra car doors being opened or doors being held open longer than necessary. Near as he could tell, John was nowhere around. They weren't sending him to stand watch in the home unless they brought him in the back which was possible, but if they did, why go through the trouble of removing their belongings? They were going to relocate the happy couple. If he was going to act, tonight might be his last chance.

Chapter Forty-Three

There's the Rub

Detective Greene walked into the room a few moments too late. The place was already turned upside down from Masterson, and he worried about what he had missed. He wanted to be there when Masterson made his way to the Guard office and tried his best to make it back in time. He'd been following up on a tip about the djinn and was certain he was close to capturing him. Then the call went out to send all of his detectives to Franklin Avenue which had been cleared days ago without further incident. That's when he headed back to the office to save Adam from the Security Director.

He could feel it when he walked through the outer door although he couldn't identify exactly what he felt. Maybe it was his own anxiety building over facing Masterson, growing until it had no choice but to permeate his own skin and dampen the air around him.

The sound of his own footsteps on the stairs echoed and bounced around in his ears. The noises built with each step he took as he reached the floor where their offices were located until his ears vibrated painfully with a harsh cycle of loud reverberations. When he pushed open the door to the conference room, everything stopped. All noise from the shuffling of files and paperwork ended as everyone froze in place, all footsteps ceased, and the murmur of voices stopped for several seconds. The only sound he could hear was his own heartbeat.

"Liam!" Masterson called out cheerfully. "Come." He motioned for him to have a seat nearby.

This wasn't the reception he was expecting. It felt like he was walking into a trap. The buzz of a busy office returned in the air around him as his staff went back to work on whatever tasks Masterson had given them. It was an odd sensation to be in his domain with a different leader calling the shots.

"Let me fill you in and explain how I've done your job for you." Masterson smiled as Liam took a seat.

'There it is. There's the rub I expected.'

Liam listened as his boss spoke. He controlled his anger while trying to seem attentive at best if not interested in what Masterson had to say. All this mumbo jumbo about patterns and clues in Mezzie's movements.

'Like we didn't already think of this!'

His men had studied the map since Mezzie first appeared at the night club hoping there would be something to give away where he and Jacoby had holed up. There was nothing. He agreed with Masterson on one point. It did seem like the outlaw genie was leading them on a wild goose chase, popping up somewhere new before the search had been completed at his last location.

"None of this matters." Masterson was saying, waving his hand across most of the city map. "The appearance at the club was to make himself known. I think we were getting too close. Where were you that night? Your men?"

"Still doing the preliminaries." Liam tried not to let the sigh be heard in his words.

"Shortly before this appearance, you were close. One of your teams were right on top of them, but missed it."

Masterson walked across the room and rifled through a couple files, more to stay busy than to look for something specific. He nodded to an aide lifting his cup in the air requesting a refill.

'Since when do we do that?' Liam's eyes widened, and he shot the man an apologetic look. It's not a part of anyone's job here to be a waitress.

"Mezzie can disguise his chem trail. Someone taught him how to cover his tracks. It doesn't dissolve it completely, but it does dramatically decrease our ability to track it. We have to be in the right spot when he shows up for us to have a chance, but he's not doing that now. He wants us to trail him. Why?"

"It's a red herring," Liam agreed. *'Tell me something I didn't already know.'*

His boss slowly walked back to the map. "All of these materializations... We shouldn't be looking there. It's a waste of resources."

"Then where should we search?" Liam was ready to end the dramatics. Masterson was known for colorfully drawing attention to his skills. It put a bad taste in the detective's mouth.

"At the beginning," Masterson said, turning to Liam. "We search where he's actually staying."

"The night club?" This was ridiculous even for Masterson.

The look on his boss' face was utter disappointment. "No," he said disdainfully. "His next stop. It was on the corner of Franklin Avenue. Franklin and..." Masterson checked his notes. "Thirty-Sixth Street. He's near there."

"We've checked-"

"Not well enough obviously," Masterson cut him off.

Liam fidgeted in his chair and grew irate listening to Masterson's explanation of why the djinn was staying in that area. It was where he materialized after leaving the club. His office had conducted an intensive search. Mezzie didn't appear again until the next day, over twelve hours later. They had made the connection he possibly stayed somewhere nearby the first night, but then he was all over the place after that.

"The location at the end of each day is within walking distance to that area." Masterson was pointing out locations on the map, reading off dates and times.

It was frustrating. Masterson was giving him a basic lesson in detecting as if he needed it. They'd search the area repeatedly without a single shred of evidence Mezzie had ever been there except for his chem trails, even less for Jacoby.

'Wait.'

"Thirty-Sixth Street. Where is that?" Liam jumped up and went to the map. He put his finger on Franklin Avenue and traced it across until it lined up with the intersection where Mezzie appeared. He continued less than two blocks farther until he saw it. "All you knead," he muttered, tapping the location of the bakery.

"What was that?" Masterson asked.

'What was it Simmons reported?' Liam paced the conference room then spied the boxes of files along the wall. He threw off the lids, skimming through the names on each folder, trying to find the R's. *'Reed. John Reed. Where are you?'*

"We need what?" His boss looked at the map confused.

It was a book. There had been a book in the apartment. "Might be a coincidence," Simmons had said. "But in my experience, there's no such thing as one."

He had told Simmons to proceed as if John was a suspect, but not too act without permission. He shook his head. *'I was certain he was wrong.'*

He lifted the lid off the next box and found the file. Everything was in there. Every detail of John's life from birth to his arrival on the surface to a copy of the business loan for the bakery. It contained everything except for the field notes for the Jacoby investigation.

"Where are Simmons' notes on John Reed?" Liam yelled to the room.

"Uh, you had me put them on your desk." A meek voice behind him answered.

Liam turned and scanned the room trying to determine who spoke.

"I'll go get them." A young woman practically ran from the room.

"John Reed. The cloaker? Will you please tell me what's

going on?"

Liam joined him in front of the board and pointed out the location again. "That's his bakery near where Mezzie appeared. His apartment isn't far from there either."

"But Reed?" Masterson crossed his arms and narrowed his eyes. "Are you sure?"

"Here." The woman reappeared and placed a stack of papers into Liam's hand.

He flipped through the notes until he found it. *'Vampires: Myth vs Truth'* written by none other than one of their own, Lilith Donovan, a vampire herself. "Positive," Liam answered.

Chapter Forty-Four

Consequences

It had taken far too long for Phillipe to leave. John hadn't bought her story about fighting with Natalie for a second. The two of them barely ever talked anymore. Their relationship had taken a hit after he and Christine started dating, but not for the reasons one might assume. He knew she wouldn't come clean about what really happened while her attacker was lurking around, pretending to be a decent guy who came to her rescue while making her feel continually threatened.

Her parents bought it hook, line and sinker. They weren't entirely in tune with Christine's life. They had a little awareness of what was going on, but were always a few beats behind.

The truth was her and Natalie had a huge falling out. They'd been friends since grade school, so the end of their relationship had consumed all areas of Christine's life for quite a while. The name hadn't passed her lips in a couple years now. If she was looking for a scape goat for the shiner on her face, she couldn't have summoned a better name.

"Good thing your friend was nearby, huh, John?" her father smirked. He didn't particularly care for John. Didn't think he was good enough for his only child, his baby girl.

John had been letting Christine down since Phillipe crashed into town, but that ended today. If her parents had any inkling of what John had done for their daughter, how she was still alive thanks to him, they wouldn't cast shade on him ever again. It was a truth which would have to remain buried lest his secrets were spilled, casting him back to the Below.

When her parents headed to bed, Phillipe finally left. As he walked toward the door, he issued his warnings. If Christine changed her story about what happened, he'd pay her another visit. The same went for if John reported him to the Guard, but she wouldn't walk away from that one. It was a promise.

As soon as the door closed behind him, he felt Christine's anger penetrate his back. He turned to her slowly and looked away as soon as he saw her face. The swelling on her left cheek along with the bruising looked more like stage makeup then the real deal even though he knew better. It was a strange mixture of amusement from how she looked like she walked into a hornet's nest and guilt from being the reason it happened which prevented him from looking her in the eye.

"Give me one good reason why I shouldn't throw you out of my life for good?" she demanded.

"Me?" he threw his hands in the air. "I didn't do this. Why did you lie to your parents? You're the one who blamed Natalie."

She folded her arms and cracked her neck. "He's *your* friend, John. You'd be guilty by association. My father would never allow you to darken his doorstep again."

He nodded while she spoke. He'd been walking on thin ice since the day he met her father. No matter what he did or how well he treated Christine, a lowly baker would never live up to the good doctor she left for him. *'Not that I've done right by her lately,'* he thought, *'but that's about to change.'*

"He's not my friend," he said in defeat.

Christine scoffed. "Yeah, I would hope you'd cut ties with him after today."

"No," John said, sitting in the chair near the sofa. "He never was." He buried his face in his hands, not wanting to get into this with her, but she deserved the explanation.

She sank onto the sofa keeping her distance from him. "Go on."

Over the next hour, he told her everything. Phillip had already opened her eyes to the world beneath the surface which made it easy for him to fill in the rest of the details. He told her how Phillipe confronted him in the bakery shortly after his arrival in Rotterdam implying he only needed a place to crash, about the Guard enlisting his help, and what they believed Phillipe's plans were with the Roth's.

"You knew he was dangerous, and yet, you didn't warn me about him?" Christine jumped to her feet and walked across the room. From where she stood, he knew she was looking at the front door, debating whether to throw him out of it.

"No, not dangerous. I didn't trust him, but I didn't think he was here for anything like this."

Christine didn't move a muscle. She continued to stand with her back to him staring at the front of the house.

John sprang to his feet and walked toward her, but when he got close, she recoiled. Seeing her react like that to him sent a current of pain from his heart to his abdomen. "You have to believe me. I really thought he was escaping the Below and needing a place to crash until things died down with the Guard before he moved on somewhere else."

"This is why you acted so strange the first time he came by." She nodded like she was figuring it out.

"I never expected him to do anything like this. I was worried about what he told you, and I was right to be. If the Guard finds out you know about us, all of us, I'll be shipped back there."

She spun on her heels and sneered at him. "How would they find out, John? Who's going to tell them? Me?"

He never thought she'd intentionally jeopardize his place here. The worry had been she wouldn't be able to act surprised if the Guard ever prepared her for integration if they married. In that moment, he half expected her to announce she was tracking them down to turn him in as soon as possible.

"Look, I'm sorry," he said. Words weren't nearly enough, but they were all he had. "I can't tell you how sorry I am. I made mistakes."

"Yeah, you did," she agreed. Her voice wavered, but he wasn't sure if it was the pain from her cheek or the pain in her heart causing the tears.

"I'm going to fix it," John promised. He inhaled deeply and nodded, reassuring himself he was making the right decision. "It's just..." He choked on his words and cleared his throat. "It's possible I'll be sent back for not reporting him right away."

"Why didn't you?" There was still anger in her voice, but it had softened enough to notice. The consequences John might face were something she hadn't considered.

John shrugged and took a couple steps away from her. With his back still turned, he said, "Phillipe helped me get to the surface. There'd have been no bakery," he sighed. "I'd have never met you. Without him, I'd be stuck underground for life."

He opened the door and paused before leaving. "If I don't see you again, it's because they sent me back. I hope you know I'll always love you."

The door closed behind him as he left, and Christine dropped to her knees on the floor. Her tears flowed freely, and her shoulders shook violently. There was no sound as she bawled. It was a result she hadn't considered. Part of her wanted to run out the door after him, screaming at him to come back, not to risk it. Part of her didn't want to ever see him again. Every fiber of her being was still in love with him and didn't want anything to happen to him.

Chapter Forty-Five

No Time for Regrets

It had been two full days since he'd seen Brendan. He had watched the foul beast of a man leave like any other day before he tended to some business with Christine. Hitting a woman hadn't been difficult at all. His whole life he never considered himself to be the type, but when it came down to it, nothing could've been easier.

The kicker was his anger wasn't with Christine. It was the worthless excuse of a man she was dating he wanted to hurt. If he allowed himself enough of a break to think things over, he probably would find he felt terrible about what he'd done, but he couldn't spare a minute to regret anything he had done to get this far. There was only the mission to focus on, and with every passing second, he moved farther away from his goal instead of inching closer.

'Where is he?'

It was possible he was in his house, sticking to the corners and hiding in the shadows. There hadn't been anyone going in or out. The only movement he could see through the windows was Serena, and even that was rare.

She had dinner in the dining room last night. There was a full view through the open front window, and Phillipe watched her eat every delicate bite of the scampi she made. She ate alone which caused him to believe the Guard might be trying to trick him into believing Brendan was gone.

More than likely, the Guard moved him. Took him somewhere to provide him better protection. *'Imagine that.'* Phillipe chuckled to himself. *'A great and powerful vampire having to hide from little ol' me.'*

Phillipe walked through the house to use the bathroom appreciating the Japanese décor along the way, holding his breath in intervals the deeper into the home he went. He smiled when he flushed and turned the faucet on in the sink to wash his hands. The only time he had cause to grin anymore was this. It's the simplest things in life which bring joy, such as having a toilet fill with clear water and being able to clean yourself with something other than a sanitary wipe.

He rummaged through the cabinets looking for more air freshener like he'd done the last several times he'd been in that room. There wasn't any of it left, and he wasn't about to go shopping for more. Once he returned to the front window and reassured himself he hadn't been gone long enough to have missed anything too important, he breathed deeply through his mouth. The smell wasn't as bad here like it was in other parts of the house near the back bedroom where the two bodies lay draped over the bed.

The only opportunity they would've had to move Roth was during his last visit to Christine's. It triggered his anger with John. The more he stewed the more he wanted to have enough time to give the sniveling weakling what he had coming. He had given John everything he had to offer, handed it to him on a silver platter, and this is what he did with it.

'A simple bakery, a meager apartment, and an average girlfriend.'

The bakery had been John's dream, but he could've moved on out of Rotterdam. There were many other places where the Guard could've sent someone like him. The success he could've had, the women, but he settled for this simpleton way of life. *'Might as well have stayed hidden beneath the surface.'*

He couldn't go to John directly. With an ability like his, the fight was never fair. Phillipe would have to take him out with the first strike. It'd be the only way to win. If John freed himself even for a second, his cloaking skills would prevent Phillipe from finding him again. It had to be Christine.

Besides, love will cause you to do crazy things. The one thing universal between both worlds was love. The way it made you feel, what you would do to get it, and the lengths you would go to protect it were the same wherever you lived. Phillipe had never been a sought after catch, but he had enough experience with women to know that much. The easiest way to control John was through Christine, but it was beginning to appear like he made the threat a little too late.

He could've missed some of Roth's comings and goings. That, or he was sneaking around through the back of the house, hoping to not be spotted, and hiding in one of the bedrooms. Phillipe had spent the last two days trying to convince himself it wasn't too late. He'd still have his chance with Roth.

'It's decided then. I'll have to make my move tonight.'

Phillipe wandered back down the hallway to Stan and Barb's bedroom. The mail he'd been collecting from behind the front door and piling on the table gave him their names. He'd picked the right house. What they lacked in air freshener they certainly made up in an interesting collection which had to be Stan's passion.

"What do you think of his fascination with swords, Barb?" he asked the grave silence of the bedroom. "May I call you Barb?"

He climbed onto the bed and carefully stepped over the couple to reach the dresser on the far side of the room. Stan hadn't gone down easily, and it was quicker than navigating the mess of overturned furniture and piles of clothes by walking around. He put his foot square on the side of Stan's head before jumping to the floor. "Excuse me, mate," he said laughing.

It was a beautiful desk top display, obviously imported. This was clearly not a mass-produced item bought on some internet warehouse. He lifted the katana he'd been eyeing ever since he barely prevented Stan from grabbing it when they met. He slowly pulled the blade out part of the way, just enough to see the hard work put into the care of maintaining it. A few drops of blood stained the tsuka which he had missed the night he put it back in its proper place.

"Did you say something, Stan?" he asked, turning back to the bed. He climbed up again to leave the room with the sword in tow. "No? I didn't think you'd object to me borrowing this again."

When he jumped to the floor on the other side, he

almost tripped over the pants legs caught under his feet. He looked in the tall stand-alone mirror still standing in the corner of the room at the grotesquely distorted mid-size figure staring back at him. He'd hunt for Roth tonight, but not without a shower first.

Chapter Forty-Six

The Book

"Ames!" Mezzie called out as soon as the customer left, walking toward his old friend with both arms outstretched.

The old man scoffed and turned his back. He busied himself adjusting the displayed items on the shelves behind the counter.

"This is how you greet friends?" Mezzie joked.

"I don't have friends," Ames answered. He came out from behind the counter and looked out the store front windows. "And you shouldn't be here."

Some things never change. "I won't be long. I wanted to ask you about the-"

"You're a threat to all of us. Why did you come to Rotterdam?"

Mezzie expected resistance, but this was a bit extreme. The only person his presence threatened was himself. "To distract the Guard while Phillipe makes his move."

Ames scoffed and shuffled back to his work. "And what move might that be?"

The way the words dripped out of Ames' mouth told Mezzie there was more to the hydrohomunculus than he realized. "He escaped the Below, yes? He needs cover to flee Rotterdam."

"And you brought it upon yourself to aid and abet a man who clearly doesn't know what he's doing, much less never asked for your assistance?"

"Look I'll be on my way in a minute. No one will ever know I was here. I wanted to ask you-"

The old man slammed his wrinkly gray hand on the counter hard enough to send a small cardboard box display filled with satchels meant to dispel evil spirits to the floor. Mezzie squatted down to pick them up for Ames while he continued his tirade. He lifted one to his nose and breathed in the scent. *'Peppermint,'* he smiled. *'Wards off pixies and fairies.'*

"You think I don't know you've been sneaking into the basement of my store every night?" Ames shouted over the counter.

Mezzie stood up, placing the box back in its place. "I haven't used my abilities here if that's what you're worried about."

"That is the only reason I haven't taken care of you for good. Materializing two blocks away. Four? Then heaven forbid you use your feet to get where you're going. Am I right? The Guard will figure it out, and they will find me in the process."

"If you would close your mouth long enough to listen, tell me where the other half of the tsavorite is, and I'll be on my way."

Ames narrowed his eyes and studied the djinn. "Why do you seek that stone?"

'Thalia.' His eyes clouded whenever he thought about her.

"To free the others." The stone had a multitude of uses, but for the time being, he wanted to free them.

"For what purpose?" Ames chuckled. "So the lot of you can run amok, terrorizing humans and our kind alike until you are all captured again? No. I won't help you in that endeavor."

The stone was here. From the second he realized Ames had a hand in dividing the tsavorite in two, Mezzie suspected he had hung onto one half. The piece he carried with him vibrated in energy ever since arriving in Rotterdam. He could feel it now pulsating in his pocket. Ames wasn't one to be underestimated. Even if the stone was locked away somewhere in this building, he could still sense its response to being so close to completion.

"Help me find Thalia." It was Mezzie's only compromise. Locating her would require both halves, and he'd figure out how to walk out of here with the full stone once she was by his side.

Ames nodded slowly, "Ahhh... That's what this is about. A woman?"

He crossed the floor of his store with a rag in his hand and dusted shelves, straightening products as though Mezzie was no longer there. "Didn't she refuse you?" he asked after a while.

A flush spread through Mezzie's cheeks. That's what everyone believed. The literal last free djinn in the world was shunned by the last female of his kind. Gives the phrase 'not even if you were the last man on earth' a whole new meaning.

"No," Mezzie groaned. "She didn't refuse me."

The old man raised his eyebrow and studied the djinn carefully. He let the gaze linger until it became quite uncomfortable, hoping it would make the pest in his store squirm.

"Why does everyone assume either of us were interested in anything romantic back then?" Mezzie blurted out. "We were being hunted. Literally being captured one by one. It wasn't the time for asking anyone on a date."

"But you did," Ames said casually, returning to his work.

Mezzie threw his arms up, opening and closing his hands into fists. Behind Ames' back, he mouthed the words and stream of obscenities he wanted to say. He had confessed his love for Thalia, and she didn't say it in return. That much was true. It was because she refused to say goodbye, believing they wouldn't be captured.

"I can see you," Ames said. He was using a stool to dust the higher shelves, facing away from Mezzie.

"I'm headed to the bakery. Would you like anything?"

"Yes," Ames said, stepping down. He turned to the djinn. "I would like for you to leave." He walked to the next section display and continued his work.

"Not without the tsavorite."

"Another favor," Ames said. "Is that what you're asking?"

"What do you want for it?"

Ames stopped dusting and stroked his beard. "What do I want? Hmm..." He pivoted toward Mezzie with mischief dancing in his eyes. "I want for you to complete your end of the bargain which is already owed to me."

'That stupid book!' If Mezzie had known the price Ames wanted, he never would've asked how to cover his chem trails.

"You've managed this long without it."

"You agreed to retrieve my book."

"I agreed to a favor! You didn't tell me what you wanted until afterward. That's on you." Mezzie was growing irate. If they weren't careful, a fight between them could lead to the destruction of several city blocks in all directions.

"I'm not going to the Below," Mezzie said.

The old man ignored him.

"Not for you or anyone," he added.

Still, Ames said nothing.

Mezzie inhaled deeply. "The bakery. What would you like?"

"I would like for you to leave my store and not return until you have my book."

"Lemon madeleines? Sounds delicious. Would you like a coffee too, *Ambrose*?"

The old man whipped around and the air inside the store circulated where the two of them stood like a personal whirlwind, stirring papers and knocking various vials and small jars over. He extended his arm fully with his palm out then brought it back, bending at the elbow. He shot his arm forward again and Mezzie slid backward out the shop door which opened for him to pass through.

Out on the sidewalk, Mezzie laughed while the door slammed shut again. He could hear the lock click, and the sign flipped over to read, "Sorry, we're closed."

"Huh." Mezzie took a deep breath savoring the aroma drifting down the street. "Guess he doesn't like lemon."

Chapter Forty-Seven

The Right Thing

Simmons and Boyd walked into the apartment of John Reed shortly after his call to the office. They had been waiting for it and were both genuinely surprised it took as long as it did. In fact, Masterson was in the process of organizing some teams fearing Jacoby got to him first.

John let them in then immediately moved to the living area and pointed to the couch. "Right here. This is where he's been sleeping." The words tumbled out like he was afraid he would lose his nerve if he didn't say them fast.

"Who?" Simmons asked. The Guard was fairly certain Jacoby had been receiving help from Reed, but they needed to hear him say it. "Who's been here?"

"Phillipe," John said. He dropped to the sofa and put his head in his hands.

The two men walked into the room and joined him. Boyd took the chair across from Reed, and Simmons sat at the far end of the sofa. "How long?" Simmons asked.

"Since his escape," John said into his hands.

Neither man could see his face, but they heard the sobs

in his throat. "Why don't you start from the beginning, John?" Boyd coaxed.

John told them everything down to the smallest detail. He emphasized how he didn't realize what Phillipe had planned. As far as he knew, it was just an escape. He didn't go to the Guard because Phillipe made threats along the way, at every turn, every time they spoke. He was afraid he'd be sent back even if he reported Phillipe right away because of the lies he threatened to tell the Guard.

Then he told them about Christine. Phillipe showed up at her house, spilling their secrets, and made it clear her life was at stake. Everything he told the two detectives was enough to send him back. He was sentencing himself to a life in cold, eerie darkness, but it was worth it if Christine would be safe.

"We know, John," Simmons sighed.

He looked at the detective surprised. "You know? Did Christine...? How?"

"We know he's been here," Boyd clarified.

John nodded and awaited his fate. It was too late. He should've come clean from the start. The outcome might've been the same, but it would've spared Christine everything she went through.

"Where is he now?" Simmons asked.

He shook his head. "I don't know. Other than briefly at Christine's earlier, I haven't seen him in days. I haven't noticed he's been back here during that time either."

"So you visited with Serena and decided to do the right thing?"

John looked at Simmons like he was speaking a different

language. "No, I just told you. He hit my girlfriend. Her face is swollen and bruised. I don't want anything else to happen to her. That's why I called you."

The detectives exchanged a look. "But after meeting Serena, you felt compelled to contact us, to come clean?" Boyd asked.

'What is he on about?' Neither of them seemed to be listening to what he had to say. The stalling was making him crawl out of his skin. He wished they would skip to the part where they told him he was being taken into custody pending review. A review, which no doubt, would send him back.

"As I told you, my only concern when you brought me home was Christine. It took as long as it did for me to get to her because I was afraid she would smell Serena's perfume on me and fear the worst, so I showered. I didn't decide to call you until I saw what Phillipe had done to her."

Simmons nodded toward the kitchen at Boyd. The two men walked several feet away and held a private conversation. Their whispered voices trickled back to John, but he couldn't make out more than the occasional word. They were discussing what to do with him. It was worth it. If they keep Christine safe of any future retribution from Phillipe, he'd go willingly. The Guard wasn't much for making deals if you believed the gossip which wound its way through certain circles, but this would be in their best interest too. It would be less cover-up for them to have to concern themselves. He might be wise to mention it when they arrested him.

"Well, Reed," Simmons said, walking back into his room.

"We're glad you did the right thing even if the road to get there was more scenic than we expected."

Simmons glanced at Boyd who nodded. "We'd like for you to come with us. There's something we need to discuss."

John swallowed hard. He feared this day would come since the notice chimed across his phone and several others in the bakery when Phillipe paid him an unexpected visit. It was time to face what was due. He stood from the sofa slowly and held his arms in front of him, wrists together, ready for them to cuff him.

'Do they use handcuffs?' he wondered. He'd never seen a Guard member with a set like the policeman wore on their uniforms. *'Surely, they had to use them. How else would they capture the ones who fought to get away?'*

"We're not arresting you, John," Boyd said. Humor could be detected in his tone.

"Put your arms down," Simmons agreed. "We're going back to the Roth's home. We believe Jacoby will make his move soon, and we want you there."

John was confused. There were repercussions. There had to be. If they still wanted his help, it had to work in his favor. His banishment wouldn't be dismissed, but maybe he wouldn't be jailed. He nodded and led them to the door.

"You did the right thing after all." Boyd was thinking out loud.

He couldn't see Simmons nod behind him. "For you, the right thing was making sure Christine was safe."

John spun around at the mention of her name and opened his mouth.

"Don't worry, John," Simmons said, holding his hands

palm out to stop him. "We've already sent a team to keep watch on her and her parents."

He exhaled slowly and opened the apartment door.

"Still, doing the right thing for you, led you back to us." Boyd chuckled. "Funny how these things work out, isn't it?"

"Indeed it is," Simmons agreed.

"What are the two of you talking about?" John was more muddled than ever.

"Serena," Boyd grinned.

"We told her we wanted you to do the right thing, but I guess now we know to be more specific. This could've backfired on us." Simmons scratched the back of his head.

"You can say that again." Boyd gave his partner a friendly hit on the back.

John simply stared at them. "What does Serena have to do with any of this?"

The two detectives smiled. Their eyes twinkled enjoying a shared secret.

"She's not simply a human, John. She's a muse." Simmons finally explained, walking out the door and down the stairs, leaving a shocked John Reed to pick his lower jaw off the floor.

Chapter Forty-Eight

In Position

"He's in position?" Masterson asked over the radio.

"Yes," Simmons voice crackled on the line. "It's just the three of them inside. Several teams are ready to move."

The two detectives had just left the Roth house after escorting Reed through the back. They had to park blocks away and enter carefully to avoid being seen by Jacoby who was hiding out in the house across the street. The couple who lived there, Stan and Barbara Wertz, were feared dead. Multiple reports about the couple had been intercepted by one of their own on the local police force.

Stan was two years away from retirement when he stopped showing up to work. None of the calls to his house or cell phone were returned, and no one answered the door. The couple was childless which was a gift to the Guard considering the mess they'd have if any of their children stopped by to check on them. A figure could be seen near the front window studying the Roth house, but he stayed far enough back to make a good view of him impossible.

Jacoby was beginning to unravel. The increased threats to John and Christine gave away his instability. Not to mention the Wertz's who were probably guilty of nothing more than arriving home at the wrong time. It'd been days since he first appeared in Rotterdam, probably longer than he'd planned to be here. The Guard wasn't sure what delayed his attack on Roth, but it played to their benefit. Perhaps that was part of it. He could believe he was out of the Guard's reach given his escape, or maybe he wanted to take out as many of them in the process as he was able.

His hesitation gave them more than enough time to prepare. They were ready. Liam was bringing the car around to drive Masterson as close as they dared to the Roth house. There had been a twinkle in his eye and a song in his voice for the better part of the day which made Liam wonder what was going through his mind.

Yes, they were close to bringing Jacoby in to custody. In all likelihood, it would be tonight. There was more to it than that. Liam got the impression Masterson felt like he was onto something the rest of them hadn't seen yet. *'It had to be Mezzie.'*

There was nothing in any of their surveillance to suggest the two were working together. It was just as unlikely the appearance of both of them in Rotterdam around the same time was a happy coincidence. Nothing was concrete as to Mezzie's involvement, but it was clear the two weren't physically together. They stayed far apart at all times. The only association between them was Mezzie was using his presence as a decoy to aid the minute criminal. Since discovering Jacoby's location and verifying it was him in the house across the street to the best of the Guard's ability, Mezzie had been on the move several times, leaving chem trail traces all over the city.

"Penny for your thoughts," Masterson said, opening the passenger door. It was difficult for him to fold his body into the car. Every moment spent on the surface had to be filled with excruciating pain for him. Pure determination brought him here, and it was the only thing keeping him around. The disguise was amazing. The average human would think he was an old man suffering from arthritis if they put their self-centeredness aside long enough to take notice of a stranger.

"Going over everything again," Liam answered. It wasn't a lie. "I want to be prepared for anything."

Masterson chuckled. "Oh, don't worry. *I* am."

Liam put the car in drive and turned out on the busy street. Something was definitely going on in that thick skull of his. It didn't make sense to withhold something from the teams putting their lives on the line to catch Jacoby. Masterson would be a safe distance away until after his capture. He wasn't risking anything, but had no problems reserving what might be vital information from the rest of them.

"Whoa," Masterson said, gripping the handle above the passenger window. "I'm excited too, but let's get there in one piece."

He eased his foot off the accelerator. He was preoccupied with Masterson's foolish antics, growing angry as he convinced himself he was right about his boss not being forthcoming, and hadn't paid any attention to how fast he was going.

"What's got you so wound up?" Masterson looked at him curiously.

Liam drummed the steering wheel and watched for traffic as he made the last turn on his way to Roth's. He couldn't tell his boss what was really on his mind. "Just eager to get this over with." He made the turn and watched the house numbers decrease as he approached. "Want to get Jacoby behind bars where he belongs."

Masterson gazed out the window like a little kid seeing something impressive for the first time. The homes in the Below were nowhere near as large as these. Or bright. "We'll get him," he said, more to a house with a white fence and child's bicycle in the front yard than to Greene. "But he won't be in your cell for long."

A shudder went down Liam's spine. There was more than one way to take that comment. Jacoby would be processed by the Guard then transferred back to the Below of course. He wouldn't be their prisoner more than a couple days at the most. No one ever was. The way the words came across, the tone in Masterson's voice made him think his boss was talking about something much more sinister.

Prisoners had a way of disappearing once they were sent back down. That information was confidential, but gossip wasn't limited to humans. Word got around easily enough, and some of it made its way back to the ears of the Guard. There'd be demerits if Masterson ever discovered any one on the team up here was sharing this information, but they looked out for each other. Everyone who made it to the Above lived in fear of being sent back. Depending on the crime, the punishment typically ended in death even if Below Security tried to pass it off as accidental.

Dusk settled around them as Liam pulled the car over a couple blocks away. Neither house could be seen through the trees lining the edges of the street. This was as close as he dared to get for now.

Masterson whipped his head from side to side trying to determine his location. When he realized he wasn't as close as he hoped to be, he objected, but Liam already had his phone to his ear.

"Simmons," the detective answered.

"It's Greene," he said, ignoring his boss's protests.

Chapter Forty-Nine

Hot Showers

It was only a glimpse, but Phillipe saw him. There was no doubt it was Roth. The coward had been hiding out in his home for at least the last couple days.

He had almost missed it. His limit for focus while staring out a window from a distance, hoping for any sign of life had long passed. Phillipe's mind would wander, and he often found himself snapping back to attention, worrying he had missed something important. That is precisely what almost happened. A few more seconds, and he'd have been out of luck.

The window to the Roth's dining room was the only one exposed. The rest of the windows on the front of the house had the curtains drawn tightly shut since Reed's visit with the enemy. This window only had valances hanging from overtop. He half expected for the Roth's, or the Guard, to cover them up with cardboard.

When he focused in on the window to the Roth's dining room after having been lost in thought for who knows how long this time, he saw him. Roth was standing there off to the left side of Phillipe's view. His entire body was visible, but his head was. There was definitely enough for Phillipe to make a positive identification of him.

It only lasted a matter of moments. Roth was talking to someone, or to himself. His mouth was moving. He turned his head and saw the window. A look of panic flashed across his face, and then he was gone.

His defenses had relaxed. He'd grown too comfortable in his fortress prepped to shield him from the man who stalked him. On this one occasion, he took a step too far into the room and stood there just long enough before realizing his mistake for Phillipe to spy him. It was all he needed.

Earlier that day, he had made the decision to make his move once darkness fell. He'd spent every minute since second guessing if it was the right course of action. Serena was in the house. That much was a certainty. If he acted at the wrong time, he may not be granted another chance. Once he was captured his days were numbered. He wasn't a fool in that regard. It was an honor to die avenging his parents. The honor would be diminished if Roth was allowed to go free, to continue living his life

There was a poetic justice to Roth being forced to live in a world where everything of value had been stripped from him. It's what Phillipe's own mother had to endure and Phillipe as well. He had toyed with that very notion since he first began formulating his escape plan in the Below. In the end, he decided to carry out justice the way it should occur, an eye for an eye.

He'd end Roth first savoring every delectable sight and sound as his life force drained from his body, preferably while Serena watched. Then he'd come for her, ending two lives at once.

Phillipe left the window for the last time and entered the bathroom. The stench was almost overwhelming now, and he coated the room with what was left of Stan's aftershave to mask it. The bottle would be empty already, but he hadn't found it until a few hours earlier. It was still full then.

The water ran in the tub until it was as hot as he could tolerate it. Running water in the Below was luke warm at best. He stripped down and stood in the tub, lifting the shower handle so the water could cascade over his body. The transformation he experienced from being exposed to so much water at once didn't hurt. It had never been painful. It was the question he'd been most asked throughout his life. When it came to his heritage, it was really the only question he'd been asked.

Well, that and how tall he could get. No one was wowed to hear his max was a little over six foot. Some humans are taller than that. The fact that he could grow about two feet by jumping in a pool didn't impress anyone. It was the only special skill attached to his kind, and it didn't set him apart from anyone when he was in that form. The colors emanating from his body did garner a few gasps and soft admiration, but it was short lived. Once he reached his full size, the light show ended. Smaller growth increments like drinking a coffee gave off such an unremarkable glow it wasn't noticeable unless the room was pitch black. There wouldn't be enough light from it to see by.

What he enjoyed most about it was watching his eye level rise. Showers were especially fun because not only did his POV grow higher, but the water's spray hit him differently as the inches were added to his body. He stayed in the stream long after the light's stopped blinding him and his body was clean. It was likely the last free shower he'd ever enjoy if not the last one period.

The odds of him walking away from the Roth house tonight a free man were not in his favor. Showers were one of the many simple things in life he'd been denied for so long. This one would be savored.

When the hot water was depleted and it became too cool for him, he finally emerged, wrapping a towel around his waist. Phillipe stared at his reflection in the mirror. The square jaw which was only prominent at his full height did wonders for his looks. This was his true form. This was how he should've spent his life.

He slipped on his clothes. They were the best fitting ones he could scavenge from John's closet and had been wearing them for days. That didn't matter. He didn't need to dress up for his own funeral. No one else would.

Phillipe checked on the house across the street one more time to see if anything had changed before slipping out the back door with the katana strapped to his waist hidden under his shirt. He wasn't as stupid as the Guard hoped he was. If Roth was in hiding, it was because they knew. Either they figured it out on their own which was doubtful, or Reed had squealed. He had stopped thinking Christine had anything to do with it. After his last visit with her, he was certain she'd never breathe a word about him if her life depended on it.

The street would be crawling with detectives, waiting

for him to make his move. He slipped out the back door, keeping to the shadows along the fence and cut through. Once he made it to the street on the back of the block, he continued heading away from Roth's house until he found what he needed.

About a mile away, he stopped in the middle of the sidewalk. *'Perfect,'* he thought.

Chapter Fifty

Crickets

John stood in the window of Brendan and Serena's dining room staring at the house across the street. It had been some time since he'd last seen any movement. The Guard was certain Phillipe would make his move soon. He'd been irrational and taking risks which meant he was unraveling, or whatever it was they kept explaining to him. None of it made much sense.

The Guard should be storming that house instead of waiting for Phillipe to come here. That was the only thing which made sense to John. It was too much of a risk waiting on Phillipe to come for his target.

Simmons felt otherwise. The objective was to take Jacoby into custody. If they stormed the house he was hiding out in and didn't get him, he'd be gone. The Roth's would forever look over their shoulders, worried he'd return to finish things one day. They needed him to come here where they were in place, waiting for him and ready for anything.

'Their only concern is catching Jacoby,' John reminded himself. *'The Roth's would be considered collateral damage if*

anything happened to them in the process. That goes for me too.'

There was some radio chatter in the next room followed by a flurry of activity. The entire house was filled with a nervous excitement except for John. He stood in place watching the Wertz residence while occasionally glancing around him as everyone scurried about wondering what happened.

He picked up a few words here and there. It was enough to get the gist of what was going on before Masterson's booming voice came over the radio. "Get the cloaker outside!"

Everyone looked side to side then at each other. None of them knew where he was, and it amused him. Even in this unimaginable situation where the lives of three people, counting the unborn babe, were on the line, John had to stifle his reaction. Once he regained his composure, he made himself visible.

"We need to move you, Reed." The voice definitely belonged to Simmons, but John wasn't sure where he was.

"Where?" John wondered out loud. The question served two purposes. *'Where are they moving me? And where are you?'*

Stepping out of the kitchen, Simmons motioned for John to join him. "Remember. We're not asking you to be a hero. You don't have to confront Jacoby."

John nodded absently. Almost every detective had been drilling it into his head since he was brought back here. He wasn't sure what he'd ever done to give these people the impression he'd try to be a hero, but he was not. That was a once and done game, and he already played it years ago.

There wasn't a person alive who could tell the tale besides himself.

"John. John!" Boyd was snapping his fingers inches from his face. "You with us?"

"Yeah," John said, furrowing his brows together. "Just got caught up in my thoughts for a second."

"There's nothing to worry about." Boyd acted like he was talking John into helping all over again.

"I know," John said.

"We'll be out there with you," Simmons added. "Once you see him, give us the signal, and we'll take it from there."

John inhaled heavily. "Yep. Where?"

"Out back," Boyd answered.

Simmons peered out the blinds in the curtains and checked his phone. "Seems Jacoby stole a truck."

"A truck!" John's eyes widened. He looked from Simmons to Boyd and back. It had taken him close to a year before he felt comfortable driving anywhere but an empty parking lot. "You're sure it was him."

Neither detective answered right away. They weren't positive. They couldn't be. The only person involved in this who could identify Phillipe in a line up when he was full height was John. It was a best guess on their part. For all they really knew, Phillipe could still be in the house across the street.

"We figure he's planning on leading us on a wild goose chase then coming at the house from the rear since we won't be expecting it." Simmons peeked through the blinds again.

"Or he'd just drive straight through the front door," John thought out loud. There were no cars in the Below. The only ways to get around were a bicycle or walking. Throughout their entire hidden world, there were only a handful of motorized vehicles, mostly for Security. Many of them never had a chance to drive before coming to the surface. Odds were Phillipe had never driven.

Both detectives' heads whipped to the front of the house like they'd never considered the possibility. Simmons motioned to Boyd who began ushering Serena away from the windows. Brendan was already hiding in a dimly lit corner where the Guard ordered him to stay. It hadn't been easy convincing him not to go after Phillipe himself, but the Guard, Masterson anyway, wanted to take Phillipe into custody alive. There had been so much talk about bringing in Mezzie too, and John tried to convince them Phillipe had never mentioned the djinn. Nothing would persuade their opinions. Phillipe couldn't have escaped without magical assistance.

"Alright, John," Simmons said. "Do your thing."

John took a deep breath and concentrated. The only change he noticed was the tunnel vision. If his eyesight wasn't narrowed by his invisibility, he'd have to check a mirror to see if it worked.

"There's several of us out here already. Boyd will join when he's through. Wander around. Keep an eye out."

He almost laughed when he remembered Simmons couldn't see him nod. "Got it."

Simmons opened the door and stepped outside, but paused long enough for John to move first. Once he was in the yard, he walked along the bushes lining the property, always keeping close to where one of the detectives was hiding. If anything changed, if any news came in, he wanted a heads up. He might not hear exactly what was taking place, but hopefully he could catch enough to figure it out. They couldn't use their radios out here, so they were using their phones carefully. The light from the screen could give them away in the darkness.

Hours passed, and there was no sign of Phillipe. The truck had been recovered miles away. It was totaled, but no sign of the driver and no witnesses. John couldn't stop yawning and was thankful none of the detectives could see how tired he felt.

The crickets quieted. The steady hum like of constant chirping had become almost soothing. He was trying to convince himself the insects hadn't gone quiet because someone was approaching when there was a loud snap behind him. John froze in place. It didn't sound like it was close by, but it sent his heart into overdrive, beating fast and goosebumps covered his exposed flesh. Within seconds, a team he wasn't too familiar with crossed the yard and left carefully through the bushes around the border.

John moved closer to where they disappeared from view, listening carefully for anything at all, but the only sounds were from the cars on distant streets. One of the agents came back through the bushes almost knocking John over. He was whispering into his phone the all clear.

It had been too close a call. There was something tugging at the back of his mind, some thought he lost or clue he missed. There was more than just the crickets. He was sure of it. He turned back to the bushes and watched for the other detective to materialize. If he wasn't careful, he'd be too distracted when the second detective appeared to avoid a collision.

Chapter Fifty-One

Crash Course

The truck was left idling on the street while the unsuspecting owner ran in the corner shop for a couple things. He'd only be a minute, and this neighborhood was pretty safe. It'd be a long time before anyone thought that again.

It couldn't be too hard. Phillipe had watched people drive in the movies shown in the Below during special events. The letters on the stick were self-explanatory. Once he figured out which pedal was the gas, it'd be easy. The rest of it was keeping the truck heading in the direction he wanted to go, and it couldn't be that hard to steer.

He had never underestimated something so direly as this. The first two seconds were the only confident moments he spent in the cab of the truck. Everything was so touchy. Putting his foot on one petal would cause the truck to lurch forward like it was trying to leave without him. The other petal brought it to a screeching halt. There was no happy medium.

It was the same with the wheel. It turned the truck too

easily. In the movies, the driver always sat with his hands gently turning the wheel side to side. This made the truck swerve left to right and back again with the tires screaming, demanding a new driver. Everyone on the street honked and yelled at him. It was already hard enough keeping the truck in its own lane, and the obnoxious remarks weren't helping his nerves.

The first accident happened on the same block he stole it. He side swiped a car parked on the street. The second accident was a bit worse. A few blocks away he nailed the back corner of a car when he ran a red light. He had to back up to get out of the intersection, and he rammed right into another car.

Beads of sweat soaked his forehead and dripped into his eyes. The saltiness burned, and his vision blurred. *'Like I need anything else making this harder.'*

He was just starting to get the hang of it. As long as he didn't have to brake or turn, he'd be fine. He sped down a residential street, making good time. There was no particular destination he was headed. He needed to draw the Guard's attention away from the Roth house if he hoped to sneak onto the property.

Phillipe blew his third stop sign in a row, but there weren't a lot of vehicles out in this part of town. Then he saw her, or at least, he thought he did. Christine was standing on the edge of the road, staring directly at him as he barreled down the street. He couldn't take his eyes off her even craning his head back at her as he passed.

Before he realized his mistake, it was too late. The truck had careened off the road, jumped the curb, plowed through a fence and was buried in some random person's front porch all the way into the front wall of the house. He tried throwing it into reverse, but it wouldn't budge. He had to crawl across to the passenger window just to climb out because neither door would open.

He ran out to the street, but she was gone. He opened his mouth to scream her name, but thought better of it. *'I know she was here. I saw her!'* Right down to her black and blue swollen face. It was Christine.

There wasn't enough time to search for her. It made him panic thinking the Guard was closer to him than he originally believed. He took off on foot, heading back toward the Roth house. Keeping to the shadows as best he could, he didn't stop to breathe until he was approaching Brendan and Serena's backyard.

The place would be thick with detectives, and he was too busy watching for where they might be hiding to pay attention to where he put his feet. He heard the snap of the large twig at the same time he felt it under his shoe. That was enough to draw them out in search of him.

Two detectives left the yard not far from where he stood in the darkness. One veered away from him, and the other passed inches in front of his face. Phillipe removed the katana from its sheath and approached the detective from the back. At the last second, he lowered his arm. If he slit his throat, he wouldn't be able to disguise himself because his blood soaked clothes would give it away. He dropped the katana to the ground, and he wrapped his arm around the detective's neck, applying pressure until he stopped fighting.

A couple minutes later Phillipe had stripped the

detective of his clothes and was ripping off the ones he took from John days earlier. He dressed quickly keeping his eyes peeled. The shoes wouldn't fit, so he put on the ones he had been wearing. All he needed was enough time to get into the house. If he could make it that far without being discovered, he'd be set.

He hid the katana under his shirt. The only weapons the detective had on him were a baton and a taser. He took those as well. The Authority didn't allow guns in the Below and expected the Guard to follow the same guidelines on the surface. Some detectives used them anyway, but he had to get stuck with one who didn't.

The phone was the last thing he grabbed. He walked to the area where the detective had emerged and held his breath while he pushed his way through the bushes. This was it.

The phone vibrated in his hand. On the screen, he could read the name Liam Greene. He was the head of the Guard. Phillipe could see the back door of the house. *So close.* He swiped his hand to answer it and held it to his ear.

"How's it look out there?" the voice asked.

Phillipe hesitated, but he held the phone to his mouth and whispered, "All clear." He ended the call before he had to speak again increasing the risk of someone not recognizing his voice. The phone vibrated again almost immediately. Another call from Greene.

The door was no more than five feet from him. He was almost there, and this phone was about to be his downfall. He kept walking not realizing how precariously close he was to Reed, almost knocking the man down when he climbed through the bushes. His breath caught in his throat until his hand was on the door knob, turning it, and pushing it open ahead of him.

Chapter Fifty-Two

Dropping the Ball

John heard the low creak of the door as it swung open when it hit him. The man who'd walked past him moments before was Phillipe. It felt like an eternity slowly eked by in the split second while his mind raced with options of what to do.

He had nothing on him. The Guard had not provided him with a weapon or a means to communicate with them. In fact, he believed the instructions he was given was, "Think of something." That's how they told him to communicate if he saw anything. Everything moved so quickly once Phillipe left the Wertz's house.

That's when they should've done their planning. One moment he was at his apartment, and the next he was here staring at the window across the street. Countless long boring hours were spent doing surveillance. They had the idea to bring Brendan into frame long enough to force Phillipe's hand, but no one was prepared for what to do next. *'Surely, they didn't expect Phillipe to walk across the street and ring the doorbell.'*

He stood in the yard feeling like he was being pulled in all directions when there was no one around him. If he revealed himself or made any noise, Phillipe would spring into action. Countless others might be harmed as well when they rushed the house after him. Taking the time to alert one of the detectives quietly provided Phillipe too large a head start, making his way through the house toward his targets. Everyone was looking for him, but no one would be scrutinizing their own people as they walked by.

In an instant, he realized there was only one choice. He ran to the door as quietly as possible and squeezed through the opening as it slowly swung shut behind Phillipe.

The two of them were face to face. Phillipe stared directly into John's eyes at one point while he finished shutting the door. John held his breath. Phillipe might not be able to see him, but he could definitely hear any noise he made. He squeezed his eyes shut for reasons unknown then forced them open. If Phillipe made a move in his direction, he'd have to be prepared.

Phillipe surveyed the house, and the detectives bustling around as they waited for updates and worked together devising plans. One nodded at him, and Phillipe dropped his head and walked toward the front of the house.

Keeping a safe distance a few feet back, John followed him. His head stayed on a swivel. The place was alive with movement, and every single one of the Guard posed a threat to exposing him if they bumped into each other. His heart thumped so hard it physically hurt, and he kept his hand on his chest trying to muffle the sound. There wasn't room in his worried mind to remember he should be alerting them the man strolling by didn't belong here.

It took less than two minutes for Phillipe to find them. They were in the spare bedroom off the front room. The Guard had stashed them there because it was out of view from the Wertz's house, gave them their own bathroom, and there were two exits. One through the front room and one through the kitchen. Phillipe had passed that one shortly after coming in the house. The door was closed, preventing him from seeing them so soon, and two detectives stood near it discussing his whereabouts.

The scene unfolded swiftly. Phillipe walked toward the room with purpose, and the guard at the door nodded at him unquestioningly. The moment John opened his mouth to yell for help, to say Phillipe's name, to scream a stream of childlike terror filled noises, anything, someone beat him to it.

A voice behind him announced, "Burns is dead."

The man standing guard straightened and walked forward past Phillipe. "What? How?"

"Seems Jacoby got to him. That's all the information I have. Waiting on updates."

Phillipe waltzed into the spare bedroom without a second glance from anyone. He pulled the katana out of its sheath from where it hid under his shirt and raised it high in the air. The unsuspecting Brendan Roth was sitting on the edge of the bed watching television with his wife. Their backs were turned to the looming danger approaching.

He brought his arm down at an angle. His aim was perfect. The blade would slice through Roth's neck. From behind, it would sever the spinal cord if not decapitate him completely. A faint smile brightened his face imagining the horror on Serena's face if her husband's head fell into her lap.

Before he made contact, Brendan fell forward off the bed onto the floor. John had failed to act since realizing who this wolf in sheep's clothing really was, but he came through when it mattered. He sprang past Phillipe, grabbing Roth, and used all of his weight to force the vampire to the floor. Then the screaming began.

"What the hell?" Brendan yelled. He was clueless as to how close he cheated death and angered someone half tackled, half pushed him off the bed.

Behind him, voices rang out in unison. Shouts of, "It's Jacoby," overlapped with orders. They called in the teams from outside and multiple confused responses like, "What is going on in there?" came over their radios. One of them he recognized as his old boss. A devilish grin sprouted on his lips. *Nice of him to take the time to come all this way just for me.*

Serena had sprung from the bed and stood in front of him, supporting the weight of her protruding belly with both hands. Phillipe lowered the blade to her midsection. A hush moved over the house. The detectives contemplated their move in silence, avoiding triggering Jacoby to act fast.

In the briefest flash, Phillipe glanced at the floor. Roth rested his arm on something not visible to anyone. It had to be Reed. He wouldn't get a second chance to intervene. Phillipe stepped forward, pulling his arm back poised to drive the katana straight into Serena, ending two lives at once.

Chapter Fifty-Three

Where Credit is Due

The Guard sprang into action, but were quickly reeled in by the booming voice of Masterson. "Let her handle this!"

Confused faces glanced at each other. Each of them searching one another, looking for a sign. The smallest inclination another detective was questioning the order, and they would have ignored the command. None of them wanted to stand by while Phillipe took the life of an innocent woman and her unborn child, but all of them wore faces of stone, giving away nothing of their true feelings.

Phillipe stared into Serena's eyes. His face full of rage. His cheeks were flush, and beads of sweat dripped down his temples. The fingers wrapped around the handle of the katana were stretched white from the intensity of his grip.

A pin drop could've been heard even with a dozen of more detectives crowded in and around the room. No one moved. No one breathed. They cast their disagreeing looks and waited.

Phillipe's arm froze mid-strike. His shoulders slumped,

but it wasn't noticed by those waiting nearby. The expression on his face fell, and his mouth dropped open. Whatever he was experiencing hadn't been anticipated.

From the floor, John saw the way Serena gazed at Phillipe, like he was a lost child. The love and compassion expressed through her eyes filled John with hope, and he wasn't the intended recipient of her power.

He stumbled just enough. His weight shifted from one foot to the other, and he leaned to the side.

A collective gasp went through the detectives. None of them expected anything of the sort. Serena was a stunning woman in her own right, but no woman in recorded history, regardless of the depth of her beauty, had stopped a crime, especially a murder, in progress.

John broke free of her spell and looked at the others. They were in shock aside from Masterson. He stood near the doorway nodding in encouragement. "That's it," he mouthed the words. John could almost hear them in his head without the powerful voice.

The katana fell to the floor at Phillipe's side, and he moaned as though releasing his grip had pained him. Before anyone could react, Masterson was already there signaling everyone to stand down.

Masterson would get the credit for this John reasoned. He showed up barely a day earlier and didn't interject too much into the plans already being set in place. His choice to use Brendan as bait, and Serena as a weapon were radical at best. The few members of the Guard who were in on the scheme weren't in support. It was too risky, but Masterson had every confidence it would work. In the end, his decision overruled everyone else.

He'd return to the Below a hero. His position in the Authority office cemented for life. The long hours the Guard put in overshadowed and forgotten. The only thing which could be better for Masterson was the capture of Mezzie, but John wasn't going to say anything.

There were rumors amongst their kind. People discussed the gossip going around regardless of who might be listening if they felt they were in a safe place. A shop like John's which catered mostly to transplants from the Below was the perfect place for them to lower their defenses. He hadn't seen Mezzie, but he had a pretty good idea of where he might be hiding. Capturing Phillipe was enough of an ego boost for the man who didn't need it.

Phillipe dropped to his knees, and John's wandering thoughts came back to the scene unfolding before him. His eyes watered and glistened in the soft bedroom light. He never broke his gaze from Serena's eyes.

Two detectives stepped softly as they closed in behind him. Any sudden movement or loud noise could break the charm she had on him. They were in position, but still they waited for the order from Masterson.

The tears in his eyes let loose, and Phillipe began to sob. Serena nodded understandingly, and cupped his chin in her hand. "I know," she whispered. "It's okay."

"I'm sorry," he cried. His gaze lowered to her swollen abdomen now at his eye level. "I'm so sorry."

The moment his eyes dropped from her hold Masterson issued the command. "Now!"

They sprang into action, grabbing Phillipe by his arms

and pulling him to his feet. Another detective secured the handcuffs on his wrists and shackled his feet. John watched in utter awe. Not all of their captures were led away like this, but Phillipe had been rather cunning.

Masterson's soft chuckle broke through the relieved air, and it made John's stomach flip. Phillipe was the bad guy here; no one else. Still, he couldn't help the growing contempt he had for the man. Phillipe deserved what he got, but this man should've stayed in the hole where he belonged.

"I'll take it from here, boys," he said after Phillipe was secured. He brushed the detectives aside and clasped one large beastly hand onto the cuffs behind his back, pulling on it hard enough to almost topple Phillipe to the ground. "I've waited far too long for this."

As Phillipe was led out, he glanced a long look in John's direction. It unnerved him, causing him to fear what repercussions Phillipe might send his way without stopping to consider how it could be done. Escaping the Below was impossible, but Phillipe managed that feat easily enough. If anyone could carry out revenge from behind bars, it'd be him.

It occurred to John he was still cloaked. No one could see him even though most of the people in the room were aware of his presence. Yet, Phillipe stared directly into his eyes. It might be luck, but it raised the hairs on the back of John's neck nevertheless.

A low din sprang up in the room. Voices overlapped, discussing what happened and what needed to be done. Most hailed Masterson as the mastermind. Through the doorway, John could see Simmons and Boyd. Their heads were down in deep conversation. If anyone understood Masterson's appearance had been more decoration than substance, it would be them.

Serena gripped the underside of her belly with one hand and leaned on the bed with the other. Brendan scrambled to his feet, supporting her. The din rose to a level of commotion best described as chaos.

John jumped to his feet and climbed over the bed. They had forgotten he was there. The sudden onset of labor pains was everyone's focus. Even Simmons and Boyd were coming to the bedroom to see what they could do.

He wasn't in the clear over his part in helping Phillipe hide out. They would soon turn their attention to him, the man cloaked from view and out of everyone's mind. This was his chance. If he was to do anything, he had to act now. He wasn't going to run. It wasn't in him. If he was to be sent away, he wanted time with Christine first. They could come for him later.

John casually walked through the front room. There were men in the kitchen, but none near the front. He opened the front door slowly, stepping through it backward while surveying the house. The only person looking his way was Serena. He noticed her as he was closing the door gently. She winked as soon as his gaze locked with hers.

Chapter Fifty-Four

Aftermath

Greene was barking orders, directing more teams' logistics than he had detectives. One team was sent to check on the progress of transporting Burn's body. Teams were assigned to both Brendan and Serena as they made their way to the birthing center where it would be determined Serena was in false labor. The news didn't come as a shock to her. She knew exactly what she was doing.

Another team was dispatched to escort Reed home, but it was discovered he had fled. They were sent to Christine's where they found him with his new fiancé on the lawn at her parents' home. He was helping her spot evidence of fairies. Events which might have seen strange a week ago didn't raise anyone's eyebrow tonight.

Several men were assigned to Mezzie detail, but it was too late. Unbeknownst to the djinn, he had picked a most opportune time to leave Rotterdam without a trace. The amount of chem trails he had been leaving behind were intentional trying to help out a fellow cryptoid. When he departed, he clung tightly to the items he needed from the apothecary. They were the real reason he visited the city crawling with Guard members. He covered his tracks completely. The residue left behind from his materialization couldn't be detected by any of their tools. Only another magical person could track him, and Ames wasn't going to rat him out.

The last two teams were sent to escort Masterson and Jacoby back to the Guard office. The pair rode in the back seat of one of the cars. When they arrived at the office, Masterson had a change of plans. He ordered one team to stay and finish any work left upstairs. They objected, but Masterson set them to task. The team driving him was instructed to take them near the windmill where Masterson had been picked up when he ascended.

Phillipe said nothing throughout the drive. He gazed out the window at the lights of the city, seeing Rotterdam with new eyes. He had blinders on during his days spent here, not appreciating what was all around him, taking it all for granted. Now his last memories of the Above, the ones which would be etched in his mind however short it may be, would be encased in darkness.

The car stopped, and Masterson demanded they join the others at the office. "We've got orders," they insisted. It was bad enough losing one team, but they weren't going to leave these two alone. Greene would have their jobs and their heads if anything happened.

"I outrank your orders," Masterson set them straight. "Get back to the office and await further instruction."

The pair walked toward the windmill. It was a little bit of a trek from where the car left them. Masterson remembered it well from his arrival. There'd be enough time for what needed to be done along the walk.

Phillipe hung his head without a word. He was heading to his execution.

"You got cocky, enjoying the hunt, thinking you were better than the Guard or even the Authority office. You thought you could outsmart us all."

Masterson was thinking out loud. He wasn't expecting Phillipe to weigh in on his reasoning. "Why didn't you go to the Roth's right away? Before anyone connected the dots?"

"Curiosity," Phillipe told him.

"I think it was more than that," Masterson wasn't buying it. "You're not a murderer, Phillipe. Not at heart. Although, you could use some anger therapy."

Phillipe chuckled.

"When it comes to draining someone's life force, that's not you. Even the Wertz's was out of necessity. They surprised you, and Stan attacked first, didn't he?"

In the dead shroud of night, he could see Phillipe nod.

"I think you needed time to let your anger stew. Enough time had passed in the Below for you to cool off. You had to build your anger again before you made your move."

Every word he was saying was true, but Phillipe didn't admit it. Nothing was going to change his fate regardless of what he had to say.

The windmill loomed ahead of them. "When does it happen?" Phillipe asked.

"When does what happen?"

"Prisoners never make it to the Below. You know what I'm talking about," Phillipe said.

Masterson laughed, fishing the keys out of his pocket. He unlocked the shackles on Phillipe's ankles. "The Roth's are being moved. Once it's discovered Serena isn't in labor, the process of relocating them will begin. They will be gone from Rotterdam by morning and will be flanked by the Guard every step of the way."

"Leave Reed alone as well," Masterson continued. "He fled believing he had a one way ticket underground right beside you, but detectives should be talking to him now. He's learning he still has his freedom."

"Your only option is to pick somewhere new and start over," he said, releasing him from his handcuffs.

Phillipe rubbed his wrists. "Are you sure about this? You're going to have some explaining to do."

"Explain what? Everyone knows being a prisoner in the Below equals a death sentence. You no longer exist as of this moment."

"Why?" Phillipe asked. He regretted asking immediately out of fear he was pressing his luck.

"The Below is dying. We're running out of resources, including oxygen. It won't be much longer until everyone is a part of the Above."

Masterson left Phillipe and climbed the stairs to the windmill's platform. He looked around into the night, taking deep breaths, enjoying the sweet smell of fresh air for the last time.

"That's it then? I can just go?" A sudden rush revitalized Phillipe when he realized he was free.

"I told you weeks ago if you got caught I'd die before I was implicated in your escape. Either you leave now, or you never get the chance again."

"Leave the others alone, Jacoby." Masterson warned him one last time. With a hand on the door, he asked him, "Any other questions?"

"Just one," Phillipe said. "Wherever did you get your hands on wolfsbane?"

More by Jennifer Lush
The Elementals Series
Air

Lilah is not at all pleased about her family's move to the Midwest regardless of the circumstances behind why they were summoned. It's unfair she has to trade in her days in the sun on the beach for the lackluster cornfields and bare trees filled autumn. Especially since it is centuries old rules and traditions dictating her family's code.

That is until she meets Jackson. The timing of events couldn't be more wrong. Secrets are revealed and psychic powers unleashed as she comes into her own while navigating the diminishing fine line between family honor and independence. Will she be able to help the other Elements fight the unknown force hunting them down while forging her own identity?

Air is the first book in The Elementals series revealing the truth behind myths and legends dating back millennia. Time is running out for the four to bring about the Return and restore Balance to the earth.

Earth

Everleigh is torn between her grandma's old fashioned ways and wanting to unite the Elementals in the fight to save their people. The vampires are being hunted, and it's only a matter of time before the unknown assailants begin their attack on the witches. Even the best kept secrets have to be revealed if they hope to conquer the storm headed their way.

New witches are being called at an alarming rate which

only solidifies what they already know. The fate that awaits them will be cold and deadly. Aligning themselves with a family of immortal psychics gathered near the town could be their only hope to succeed in the fight for survival. Will she be able to help convince the factions to join together in time?

Earth is the second book in The Elementals series revealing the truth behind myths and legends dating back millennia. Time is running out for the four to bring about the Return and restore Balance to the earth.

Fire

Judd is torn between two identities. The private life he leads has to remain a secret. It's the only way to save his son. The life he's known by is a past filled with carnage and intimidation. His people are being hunted, and he has to figure out a way to save them without putting his family at risk.

There was a time when vampires roamed all corners of the earth doing as they pleased. Too many times, hunts raged to murder the foul beasts that existed with the humans. The Council created rules that would keep order amongst the clan preventing future onslaught, but now the Council was being targeted as well. Will Judd find who is behind these attacks before the entire clan has fallen?

Fire is the third book in The Elementals series revealing the truth behind myths and legends dating back millennia. Time is running out for the four to bring about the Return and restore Balance to the earth.

Ravenwood: Volume One

Along Route 116 where the state road weaved its way through the backwoods of Massachusetts was the lane leading to Ravenwood. It was easy to miss. The only travelers in that area were either lost or looking for the old Europeanesque inn. The only people who traveled west of Ravenwood were the people who had grown up there. They knew the woods, feared the creatures who dwelled there, but they respected them. They had made friends with the woods for it were the trees who wouldn't let you leave.

Available on Kindle Vella
Ravenwood: Volume Two

Pick up where you left off with more short stories about Ravenwood! Along Route 116 where the state road weaved its way through the backwoods of Massachusetts was the lane leading to Ravenwood. It was easy to miss. The only travelers in that area were either lost or looking for the old Europeanesque inn. The only people who traveled west of Ravenwood were the people who had grown up there. They knew the woods, feared the creatures who dwelled there, but they respected them. They had made friends with the woods for it were the trees who wouldn't let you leave.

The Elementals: Water

The Elements were spiritual entities behind the veil until they materialized corporeally to experience human life. One year was the time frame they were allotted, but it stretched into centuries. Their undoing is at hand, but they must first find out who is trying to bring them down. Water follows the fourth Element's journey from the other side to the beginning of the fight for her kind. Will the Elements finally be able to put their past behind them to fight for their lineage's survival?

The Below: Seasons One and Two

All manner of supernatural and mythical beasts dwell in The Below. Their refuge underground has kept them safe for centuries. Their world is failing and more of their kind are ascending to the surface. Season one follows Phillipe. He had always known he would never go to The Above. He was the last of his kind, and he hadn't always followed the rules. He accepted this as his fate until he learned the truth about his parents. Their murder and the lies that covered it up sparked an outrage. There was only one way justice would be carried out, and that was by Phillipe's own hands. Season two tracks Mezzie's quest to save his own kind, free the love of his life, and get to the bottom of Ambrose's involvement in his betrayal of the djinns.

Fogpoint Harbor

Kat was surprised to learn of her great-aunt's death twenty years after she had been led to believe Aunt Dot had passed away. As the soul inheritor of the estate, there was a catch. She had to live in her aunt's house for one year to collect. The mysteries surrounding her aunt didn't end with why she had been lied to about her death. Recruited by the police to solve a town's murder, Kat relies on an unlikely source to solve the crime: the ghosts residing in her aunt's Victorian home.

About the Author

Jennifer Lush is a mother of three from central Illinois where she has lived her entire life. Aside from spending time with her children and grandchildren, writing and traveling are her two main consuming passions. Luckily, they are mutually beneficial.

Writing has always been in her blood even if it took her longer than planned to do it. One of her earliest memories of longing to be an author happened in kindergarten when she told her parents what she wanted to be when she grew up. It took close to four decades, but she has finally made that childhood dream come true.

Jennifer is an entertainer at heart who is always making those around her laugh. She can turn any mundane event into a story worth repeating with flair. Inspiration for her fictional worlds comes from everywhere. There are more ideas floating through her mind than she has time to write, but she is determined to finish as many as possible.

Twitter: AuthorJLush
IG: AuthorJenniferLush
Tik Tok: AuthorJenniferLush